I've travelled the world twice over,
Met the famous: saints and sinners,
Poets and artists, kings and queens,
Old stars and hopeful beginners,
I've been where no-one's been before,
Learned secrets from writers and cooks
All with one library ticket
To the wonderful world of books.

© JANICE JAMES.

THE REJECTED SUITOR

Lady-in-waiting Kira Chirnov has fallen in love with Alexis, the brother of the mistress of Tsar Alexander II. However, Kira's brother, Sergei, poisons her mind against Alexis so that she rejects his proposal of marriage. Alexis is too proud to admit he took the blame for Sergei's card-cheating and determines to think no more about a girl so easily swayed by an unscrupulous brother. When Kira learns the truth, she finds it is not easy to win her suitor back.

MARGARET STEWART TAYLOR

THE REJECTED SUITOR

Complete and Unabridged

ULVERSCROFT
Leicester

First published in Great Britain in 1982 by
Robert Hale Limited
London

First Large Print Edition
published July 1994
by arrangement with
Robert Hale Limited
London

British Library CIP Data

Taylor, Margaret Stewart
    The rejected suitor.—Large print ed.—
Ulverscroft large print series: romance
I. Title
823.914 [F]

ISBN 0–7089–3122–7

Published by
F. A. Thorpe (Publishing) Ltd.
Anstey, Leicestershire

Set by Words & Graphics Ltd.
Anstey, Leicestershire
Printed and bound in Great Britain by
T. J. Press (Padstow) Ltd., Padstow, Cornwall

This book is printed on acid-free paper

1

FOR early October the weather was unusually mild, yet some days ago, when Kira Chirnov was in the Petersburg Summer Garden, she had noticed workmen engaged in boarding up the classical statues. This was done every autumn to protect them from the severe cold of winter in accordance with an order laid down by Tsar Peter the Great more than a century and a half earlier.

Kira assumed the annual task would have been completed now, so it surprised her to see, on the other side of an artificial pond, a man in a rough sheepskin coat with scarf on his head, seemingly dragging back part of the wooden cover round one statue. The distance across the water prevented her from seeing the operation clearly until he got inside the cover, pulled it back into position, and was then hidden.

When creating the city of Petersburg,

Tsar Peter the Great laid out the Summer Garden. In theory it was a public park where all might wander, but only the wealthy had leisure to do so, and this afternoon the place seemed deserted. Once past the entrance gates Kira had seen only the single workman.

The present Tsar Alexander II used it for regular morning exercise when in Petersburg, since his official residence, the Winter Palace, had no proper garden. Sometimes attended, but often alone, he would stride along the formal lanes lavishly bordered by trees, now leafless. The fountains were turned off. As for the classical statues they looked grotesque with their protective covers.

Why had a workman disappeared like that? Curiosity attracted Kira Chirnov and she made her way to the statue. She could not go across the artificial pond so had to follow a path round it, and thus examine the covered statue from the front.

Although Kira was eighteen, nearly nineteen, not much of her life so far had been spent in Petersburg, and the Summer Garden was still a novelty to her. She knew she was defying convention to walk there alone, but after seeing off her sister-in-law to Moscow, she felt the impulse to enjoy an unaccompanied wander, just as she had been able to do at Barona, her father's country estate.

Deaf to the protests of the coachman Mischa, Kira had countermanded the order from Princess Lydia, her brother Sergei's wife, to take her to Count Chirnov's house. Mischa was to drive to the principal gate of the Summer Garden and wait there for her.

"I shall be walking in the Garden for quite an hour." And when reminded the afternoons were drawing in, she said she should have returned to the carriage before the light had begun to fade.

As she walked she let her thoughts ramble and, as was quite usual, they reverted to the country where she had spent the most impressionable years of childhood, and would never forget. It was now called Alaska, but had once been Russian America. Russia, having no use for it, sold it to the United States, and during the protracted negotiations Count Chirnov was sent there to conduct them.

Kira was a mere two-year-old when she accompanied her parents on the long journey across Siberia and the Bering Sea. The only remaining member of the family was her older brother Sergei, and at fourteen he was in a preliminary military training school, due later to enter the honoured Preobrajenski regiment. Such a future could not be interrupted by several years in Russian America, but a girl like Kira could be governess-educated. It was the same when her father returned to Petersburg seven years later, then to be made Russian Consul in Salonika where he again took wife and daughter. Sergei had now married the Princess Lydia Granovski.

Count Chirnov was relieved of this post because of his wife's illness. He took her to Italy for treatment, but after months of lingering she died. Meanwhile Kira went to school for the first time. The exclusive Smolny Nobility School for Girls in Petersburg was a boarding establishment run on spartan lines like a convent, and aristocratic birth was essential for entry. The Tsar and Tsarina were its patrons. They paid regular visits of inspection, and

Kira Vassilievna Chirnov was singled out for special notice because Alexander II held her father in high esteem for his diplomacy in Russian America and the secret service side of his duties in Salonika.

Kira hated the dullness and confinement of the Smolny. None of the other girls was interested in her unusual travel experiences so she withdrew into private dreams of the former Russian colony, the long journey across Siberia, and the totally different experience in Salonika. This part of northern Greece belonged to the Ottoman Empire and here Kira became aware of tension between Mohammedan rulers and oppressed Christian subjects. There was none of the freedom for women she had taken for granted.

She should have made her debut in Petersburg society after reaching her seventeenth birthday, but the Countess Chirnov's death necessitated a year of mourning — at least for the Count and his daughter. Sergei was expected to continue his military duties. Despite grief for Mama, Kira loved the free informal life on the Chirnov country estate. However, it distressed her to observe her father's continued grief.

"I have no stomach for Court now," he told her. "In September I shall send you back to Petersburg to live with Sergei and Lydia. She will introduce you into society."

Princess Lydia, the sister-in-law, was of nobler birth than the aristocratic Chirnov family, and was already an important hostess. Also, she and Sergei were favourites of the Tsar's Heir Apparent, the Tsarevich, and his Danish wife. Secretly Kira dreaded 'coming out', and wished she could remain at Barona, growing closer to Papa and in time getting him to take an interest in life again.

Then one day a letter arrived from the Tsar. Kira was practising a musical piece when Count Chirnov walked into the room, holding a thick sheet of paper covered with small writing above which her eyes saw the double-headed eagle, emblem of the tsars.

In quite an animated voice he said, "His Imperial Majesty wants me to undertake another delicate mission abroad next spring."

6

Kira had risen to her feet and was facing him in excitement. Could it be the country she so loved in childhood?

"Is it in Russian America, Papa?"

"My dear child, Russia rid herself of that colony after traders had nearly exterminated most of its valuable fur-bearing animals, and I certainly took my share in ensuring my country made a satisfactory sale to America. No, the Tsar wants me to go to a country newly independent of the Turks, but needing the overriding influence of Russia for some time to come. Otherwise Austria, Prussia, even England, will step in."

Turks! A place like Salonika!

"Is it in the Balkans, Papa?"

"Yes, my dear, Bulgaria."

Seeing the blank perplexity on his daughter's face, Count Chirnov briefly explained how Bulgaria had become independent after centuries of oppressive Turkish rule, an independence achieved by Russia to whom the new state turned for advice. Already the Tsar had been asked to choose their first ruler, who must be a foreign prince; and Alexander had selected his nephew, Prince Alexander of Battenburg. Unfortunately he had not been trained in statecraft, so needed, as Count Chirnov expressed it 'a guiding hand', and that hand was to be the Count's.

Kira was deeply disappointed to discover her father was not intending to take her with him, since the debut in Petersburg society was all-important. The only consolation was that since her father now decided to leave Barona straightway and re-open the Petersburg mansion, she would be residing there, instead of with Sergei and Lydia, until Papa went to Bulgaria in the spring.

Kira adored her brother. She tried to be fond of his wife, but shrank from Lydia's autocratic, domineering behaviour, and resented her powerful influence over Sergei. Although just thirty, the latter was now a captain in the Imperial Life Guards, the Preobrajenski. Kira was expected to be as successful in the role assigned to her — that of social belle to whom numerous suitors would offer marriage because of her high birth, large dowry, and good looks.

Certainly Kira was pretty, with glossy

raven hair, large dark eyes, and a slim, graceful figure, but the months at Smolny had given her a nervous dread of being a failure in this etiquette-ridden world to which she was now being introduced. Society and marriage were the two chief topics of conversation among her fellow pupils and Lydia's haughty sophistication increased Kira's lack of confidence for Lydia came of the noble Granovski family. The marriage to Sergei, delayed until the return of Count and Countess Chirnov from Russian America, had greatly pleased the bridegroom's parents. Later came the Countess's illness, followed by her death. Another victim of the same complaint was Tsarina Marie, wife of Alexander II, at present undergoing treatment for tuberculosis in the south of France. Kira had met her twice when the imperial couple visited the Smolny, and was impressed by her kind manner but could hardly believe she had once been beautiful. Ill-health had robbed the Tsarina of her looks. Later Kira heard there was another reason, that the Tsar no longer loved her.

In spite of disappointment at not going to Bulgaria, Kira rejoiced at the beneficial effect the prospect of this commission from the Tsar was having upon her father. After saying he would not come to Petersburg for his daughter's debut but leave everything to Lydia, he changed his mind, reopened the town house, and even attended Kira's first ball. Social life for Kira was halted through Lydia's being summoned to a sick relative in Moscow. Sergei was already on army manoeuvres near there.

Kira's shyness had not contributed towards her success at that ball and her sister-in-law grumbled at her afterwards.

"You must do better when I return, or getting you well married is going to be very difficult for me."

These were Lydia's parting words, and Kira experienced a sense of relief as the Moscow-bound train left. The feeling of being reprieved, though only for a short time, had caused her to indulge in this solitary walk in the Summer Garden.

She was beginning to think she might be the only person enjoying the park, but as she came round the pond, she saw a group on a stretch of grass beyond the statue she was aiming for. The grass was still free of even light snow. A small boy and girl and a tall man were chasing each other round a group of fir trees, while two obvious nursemaids stood waiting until required, and a lady beside a bent alder tree was calling encouragements to the chasers. Kira approached cautiously. She wanted to reach that statue without being noticed, but did not know how she should achieve this. To consider the matter, and at least watch the front of her objective for she was fairly close to it now, she hid in crouching position near a small bush.

Now the group changed to what was clearly a game of hide-and-seek. The gentleman leant against one of the fir trees and shut his eyes. The two children ran off, after whispering to the lady. She returned to the bent alder tree, and as it was not far from the statue she would see if Kira emerged from the bush. Kira had a good view of her and now realised who she was. The memory of an incident happening only yesterday returned. Lydia and Kira were driving along the Nevsky

Prospect when traffic was slowed down by some obstacle in front. Coming in the opposite direction was a carriage. In it sat the lady now by the alder tree and two children, evidently the same as those playing hide-and-seek. Lydia had given an angry snort of contempt.

"That disgraceful creature and her bastard offspring!"

"Who are they?"

"Were you so cloistered at the Smolny that you never heard of the Princess Catherine Dolgoruky?"

"There were rumours passed among senior girls," admitted Kira. "Yes, I have heard the name and how she let the Tsar install her in a house on the English Quay. I suppose he visits her at that house."

"It is far worse now. His Imperial Majesty has brought her into the Winter Palace itself. True, she is isolated in a private suite and the Tsarina has no connection with her, but the indignity is disgraceful. A mistress under the same roof as a wife! If a man has *chères-amies*, he does not act so indiscreetly even though he be the Tsar, and this present

12

situation shocks us all. The Tsarevich and the Tsarevna are horrified."

"Does the Tsarevich protest?"

"To his father, the Tsar! You know no subject dare criticise any action of His Imperial Majesty openly, but a great deal is said in private."

By the words 'in private', Kira gathered Lydia meant that the scandal was discussed everywhere save before the monarch.

"Sergei is absolutely faithful to his marriage vows," added Lydia complacently.

Now in the Summer Garden, looking at the Princess Catherine Dolgoruky, Kira wondered what would eventually happen to her and her children. So absorbed was she in conjecture that she forgot about the workman and the statue. Then some strange premonition of fear brought back her attention to this puzzle. The Princess was watching for the return of the hide-and-seek players, so with her face turned the other way, Kira decided she could walk to the statue, examine it and see what the workman was doing, and after that take a path round the other side of the pond. Princess Dolgoruky, if she saw her, would know Kira had a right to be strolling in the Garden like any other member of the public.

But before she actually reached the statue, one of its wooden covers fell to the ground, only just missing Kira who hurried to reprove the workman. He must have knocked it down, but he should have made certain nobody was close and liable to be hurt. He seemed oblivious of her approach. Then she saw his right arm was raised and that the hand attached to that arm was clutching a revolver. Roused to action, she rushed forward and struck the man as he fired, her unexpected violent blow catching his elbow and deflecting his aim. Otherwise the bullet would have struck the Princess, but it fell short of its target, burying itself harmlessly in the grass.

The assassin turned in fury on Kira, whom he had not seen before, and she quailed before his blazing eyes. In an educated voice he abused her for interfering with justice, an accusation which made her think he must be one of the Nihilists she had heard about.

They were a band of fanatics pledged to kill the Tsar and all connected with him. She struggled as he seized her, sickened by the smell from dirty clothes such as a workman would wear — though he was certainly no workman, but his grip slackened and she realised another man had come to her rescue. Everything went misty as she collapsed and fell to the ground.

In spite of a blow on her forehead, Kira regained consciousness in a short time, and her first impression was of noise and people in that hitherto quiet park where visitors were few. Now she saw uniformed police dragging away the assassin who was shouting and cursing. She herself was lying on the grass with her head resting on a hastily contrived pillow. Standing over her was a tall man cloakless and it dawned upon her he was the one playing with the Dolgoruky children. He had worn a cloak then. He must have taken it off to fold up and use as a pillow for her aching head. She wanted to thank him, certain it was he who had rescued her from the Nihilist, but his blue eyes and handsome tanned face whirled mistily as she tried to fix her own dark grey eyes on them.

"Where have these police guards come from?" she asked and the cloakless man bent down.

"It is all right, Mademoiselle. The murderer is being taken into custody."

"But there seemed to be no officials about the Garden."

"There were and a search was started for you. A coachman waiting at the chief gate had become anxious . . ."

"Oh, Mischa!" Kira said. Assisted by the stranger, Kira struggled to her feet, assuring him she was better, although she was too dizzy to do so without his supporting arm.

"If you have a carriage waiting, allow me to carry you to it. You are not fit to walk. You must go home and rest."

"I shall be all right after a rest," murmured Kira mechanically, wishing her head hurt less.

At this moment, two policemen came holding Mischa the coachman. He looked terrified, as were all ordinary folk, of officialdom. Kira hastened to identify him. She was too grateful to him for

16

raising the alarm about her whereabouts to be vexed over his thus disobeying her commands.

She said, "This is my father's coachman. I ordered him to wait by the garden gates while I enjoyed a stroll by myself. Fortunately he seems to have become alarmed and spoken to an official."

The stranger still supporting her explained how police, suspecting a Nihilist had entered the Summer Garden with murderous intent, questioned the waiting Mischa 'and my sister's coachman.'

So this man must be brother to the Princess Catherine Dolgoruky! She looked round, but there was no sign of the lady, children, and nurses. A police officer, obviously the man in charge, addressing the Prince as Highness, enquired the name of Kira's father and where he lived in Petersburg. Kira herself supplied these particulars. Mischa's story was accepted without further questioning. Then the Prince announced he would escort her home and he wrapped the long black cloak he had used as pillow around her.

"To whom am I indebted for your

kindness and for rescuing me from that Nihilist before he killed me in his rage?" she asked.

"Prince Alexis Michailovich Dolgoruky, at your service, Mademoiselle."

He wanted to carry her to the entrance gate and at first Kira refused, but before they were halfway round the pond she was obliged to allow him to take her up in his arms. He carefully assisted her into the carriage and seated himself beside her while Mischa took his place in the driving seat. A groom who had been holding the horses scrambled up as well. Leaving, Kira noticed they were followed by two mounted police guarding them.

On arrival all was confusion. Kira insisted that she was capable of walking upstairs to her bedchamber, but she did feel in need of rest so hoped Prince Alexis would excuse her retiring instead of entertaining him. A footman had already explained her father was out, but expected back within the hour.

"If you have no objection, Mademoiselle, I will wait for Count Chirnov and tell him about this afternoon's incident. When you are better I know my sister will wish to thank you for the great service you rendered in saving her life. Yes, you did, Mademoiselle. It was your bravery that caused the assassin's bullet to miss my sister."

Kira enquired if the Princess and her children had left the Summer Garden safely.

"They were straightway taken back to the Winter Palace under police escort." Prince Alexis did not seem ashamed to mention Princess Dolgoruky's residence. He added, "I am afraid the happy walks in the Summer Garden, so enjoyed by them, will be restricted in future."

The lump on Kira's forehead was throbbing painfully, also she was feeling the bruises from the assassin's rough handling. She longed to be free to relax and to be petted by Anna, her mother's maid, but she was sufficiently mindful of hospitality duties to give orders for the Prince to be served with refreshments while he waited for her father. Then she bade him good-day. He kissed her hand in polite fashion, bowed, and was taken into the drawing-room by a servant.

Once in her bedchamber, Kira thankfully

submitted to Anna's care and fussing. She would have been surprised to know how Mischa was spreading news of the incident in the kitchen regions. The whole household soon knew how Kira Vassilievna had saved the mistress of the mighty Tsar from a Nihilist who tried to kill that notorious . . . he used a distinctly uncomplimentary word for Princess Catherine Dolgoruky. Like all senior servants, he referred to Kira by her christian name and her patronymic. Vassilievna meant daughter of Vassili, that being the Count's name. Prince Alexis had called himself Michailovich Dolgoruky, that is son of Michael Dolgoruky.

Bathing and application of soothing ointment eased the pain of her forehead, and it was bliss to lie between cool sheets. Kira soon fell asleep. It was some hours later when she awoke and, for a moment, was bewildered to see her father sitting by the bed. He was looking at her anxiously as she opened her eyes. She hastened to reassure him that the would-be assassin had done her no real harm.

"Prince Alexis Dolgoruky was staying

to tell you all about the affair, Papa."

"Yes, he told me how you saved the life of his sister, the Princess Catherine Dolgoruky, when a Nihilist attempted to shoot her in the Summer Garden."

There was a note of embarrassment in the Count's voice as he spoke of the Tsar's mistress and Kira was surprised he even mentioned the lady's name. It was one thing for Lydia to supply information about a scandalous situation, but different for Count Chirnov. Then Kira understood when he remarked that the head of the Secret Police, General Trepov, would be calling to ask her for her account of the attempted assassination.

"But not until you have recovered from the shock, my dear. That villainous Nihilist is in prison and will, in due course, be executed."

"Papa, are there many of these Nihilists? What do they want to achieve?"

"General Trepov was supposed to have rounded them all up. He thought there were only a few, but there must be a greater number than estimated. They are fanatics and are educated, not mere

21

peasants. Oh, they want various social reforms."

"But the present Tsar is a reformer. Look how he freed the serfs. What more can he do?"

"Thousands expect more than that but are aware of the time social changes take. Not the small circle of Nihilists, who declare their political aims can only be achieved through murder. Any of them at large are sworn to kill the Tsar and those connected with him."

Again Count Chirnov looked awkward. "Possibly you have not heard of the Dolgorukys before today?"

Taking Kira's silence for a negative, he went on, "They are one of our oldest noble families, descended from Rurik himself. The late Prince Michael Dolgoruky was a personal friend of His Imperial Majesty, who became guardian to the children when orphaned. They were left comparatively poor since Prince Michael had been absurdly extravagant, even mortgaging the family estates at Poltavia in the Ukraine; but the Tsar put the sons in the army, in the Preobrajenski or in training for it, and the two daughters he sent to the Smolny. Oh, both must have left long before you were a pupil, Kira. This son who brought you home is the youngest and he is about Sergei's age."

"I know I should have entertained him, Papa, but I was feeling so unwell then."

"Prince Alexis quite understood that, my dear. He was most concerned about you and asked my permission to call and enquire after your health tomorrow. Naturally he does not expect to see you until you are better. I have summoned a physician. You have had a shocking experience."

"It was nothing. I am thankful the Nihilist did not kill anybody."

"Prince Alexis said the bullet was aimed directly at his sister, only you pushed the villain's arm and it did not strike her. When you have recovered the Princess Catherine Dolgoruky wishes you to come to the Winter Palace so that she can thank you personally. The Tsar is in the Crimea, but I expect he will thank you on his return."

The Count was speaking plainly. Kira

realised he was assuming she knew the facts of the situation. To ease matters she asked if Prince Alexis Dolgoruky knew Sergei since he was in the Preobrajenski.

"No, Prince Alexis left the regiment as a very young man. The Tsar found he preferred academic to military studies, was most understanding, and permitted him to resign and instead attend a university abroad. There he became interested in astronomy. He is an astronomer and works now at Pulkova Observatory."

Kira knew Pulkova was only ten miles from Petersburg, that it had a famous observatory, but that was all. It amazed her that the Prince should want to be an astronomer.

"What exactly does an astronomer do, Papa?"

"Prince Alexis told me he was chiefly concerned with observing movements of stars. I had heard His Imperial Majesty took a great interest in the observatories of both Pulkova and Petersburg, but Pulkova is newer and far more important."

"How extraordinary! Does Prince Alexis spend any time at Court, Papa?"

"None at all, I gather. He is a scholar, not a courtier."

Kira thought that precluded him from being among the suitors Lydia would be selecting for her.

2

MUCH as she hoped to receive Prince Alexis when he called next day, Kira found this impossible. The physician summoned by her father insisted she remain in bed for the rest of the week.

"And I should think so, Kira Vassilievna," declared Anna, the elderly servant who had been personal maid to the late countess, and who spoke to her present mistress as if Kira were still a little girl. "You were quite feverish last night and calling out in your sleep because you were delirious."

"I had a nightmare, but I am all right now."

However, when handed a mirror Kira was forced to admit that the lump on her forehead looked dreadful and the eye below it was black. The assassin certainly struck hard. No, she would prefer to look her normal self before being seen by an outsider. Later her father came to tell her the Prince had called though he had now gone.

"He was very concerned about you. So is the Princess Dolgoruky, and she has requested him to bring you to her private apartments at the Winter Palace when you are sufficiently recovered. She wishes to thank you in person."

Observing his daughter's surprised look, count Chirnov no longer doubted she was acquainted with the notoriety attached to the lady who was condemned by Petersburg society in general.

He said, "It would be inadvisable to mention any Winter Palace visit to Sergei and Lydia. The Tsarevich feels for his mother, the Tsarina Marie. He dare not express disapproval direct to the Tsar but plenty is said at the Anitchkov Palace, especially by those who court favour with the Tsarevich and the Tsarevna like your brother and his wife."

"But what do you think, papa?" asked Kira, astonished at her own daring.

"The Tsar is ruler of All Russia. He has been placed in that position by Almighty God. Therefore criticism of his actions by his subjects is wrong."

The solemnity of the answer impressed Kira. If that was what Papa believed, then she followed Papa.

"Well?" unexpectedly queried Count Chirnov.

Rather confusedly Kira remarked that Prince Alexis must be on friendly terms with Princess Catherine since he had been playing with her children in the Summer Garden, but what about the rest of the Dolgoruky family?

"There are several older brothers and one sister, Princess Berg, who is married to the Viceroy of Poland's nephew. They all ignore Princess Catherine, following the general practice of Petersburg society. This is due to the Tsarevich and his Danish wife, the Tsarevna." Angrily Count Chirnov added, "I disapprove of Sergei and Lydia being so much at the Anitchkov Palace. Even if the Heir Apparent will one day be Tsar, while Alexander II lives and reigns, he is my Tsar. I fawn on no rising star of the future."

Silently Kira was in agreement, although she herself felt sympathetic towards the injured Tsarina Marie whom she had met with the Tsar at the Smolny. Marie's children must pity her plight.

Male members of the Imperial family were expected to make marriages of convenience, diplomacy overriding love, though Alexander II, when he was Tsarevich and Heir Apparent, fell violently in love with Princess Marie of Hesse; but the duchy of Hesse was too unimportant to satisfy the ambitions of his parents, and at first they refused consent. Alexander persisted until they gave way. The marriage was happy and he a faithful husband for many years, but Marie's health was ruined by childbearing. He sought other distractions, eventually conceiving a *grande passion* for a girl nearly thirty years younger than himself. She was Princess Catherine Dolgoruky, and his ward.

For some time Catherine resisted his advances, even trying to escape from him by staying with relations in Italy. Then she yielded. For thirteen years the two had been lovers, and though the affair was kept secret at first, it soon became known publicly. Alexander took a house for her on the English Quay and visited her there. Later she moved to the Winter Palace where she had private apartments and lived in seclusion. She never appeared in society. If the Tsarina Marie were in Petersburg, and well enough she took her place at any function by her husband's side, as rigid etiquette demanded. Otherwise the Tsar would be followed by just two aides-de-camp.

Prince Alexis continued to call daily and enquire after Kira's health, but only her father saw him. The Count had taken a fancy to the young man and was very interested in his astronomical work at Pulkova, so she gathered. Amid all the confusion of that day in the Summer Garden she was left with a blurred picture of his appearance. She was curious to see him again, though convinced she should never be able to talk to him with any understanding of astronomy as Papa evidently could. Beyond having heard of Pulkova Observatory as a place of great importance she had no idea of the work accomplished there.

Her first visitor allowed by the physician

was, however, the head of the Secret Police, who wanted a detailed account of how the odd behaviour of the workman attracted her attention, up to his attacking her when she caused him to misfire. General Trepov presented an inexpressive face to Kira, but inwardly he was terrified the incident might lose him his high position. He had boasted to the Tsar, before the latter last left Petersburg, that he was confident the Nihilist movement was shattered. Certainly the General had had leaders and some followers executed, the remainder going in chains to Siberia with life exile before them. Yet it had not been enough.

Under repeated questioning in prison, the disguised workman proved to be a Nihilist idealist whose superiors assigned him the duty of killing the woman so dear to the Tsar. That was a mere preliminary to the same superiors killing the Tsar, only how this was to be done examination of the prisoner failed to elicit. It was clear he did not know. He was due for execution after General Trepov had interviewed Kira, but, as was feared, her testimony gave no help. The

31

General returned to his headquarters very worried. He had already sent warnings to Moscow and Livadia for extra precautions to be taken while the Tsar remained in the Crimea and on his return journey to Petersburg.

Even a short spell at the Smolny Nobility School had given Kira poise. Shy as she was by nature, she automatically walked into a room and greeted people in a manner appropriate to their station. At school this had been called 'circling'. Chairs were set out bearing names of imaginary aristocrats. The pupil went round, making an appropriate remark to each, and her efforts were criticised by the teacher. Thus, when the physician had pronounced Kira to be fit and a summons came from Count Chirnov that he wanted her in the drawing-room, she entered nervously, yet with confidence enough to greet Prince Alexis and thank him for saving her from the Nihilist's rage.

"Indeed, Mademoiselle, it is I who am in your debt. But for your courageous action that villain would have killed my sister."

He went on praising Kira while she

studied the face she had not been able to look at properly when they met before. It was the eyes that impressed her because they reminded her of somebody else she had seen, but who or where she had no idea. They were dark blue and they had an unusual glitter, slight but striking. They also gave the impression of looking far ahead, a result of peering through a telescope at stars, decided Kira. Perhaps he was not really handsome, though he was certainly attractive. He was tall and he stood with a carriage as erect as any drilled soldier's similar to Sergei's. She liked the sound of his voice. It was grave and low-pitched. Oh, he was an impressive person, especially with those eyes that tantalised her. She was positive she had seen another man with eyes like those, and it was absurd how the memory eluded her.

Prince Alexis proved adept at conversation, touching lightly on ordinary topics without reference to his astronomical work, and her father talked with an animation Kira had not seen from him since her mother's death. The visitor rose to take his leave after the correct time for a social call was ended, and then he mentioned his sister's desire to thank Kira. When might he have the honour of taking her to the Winter Palace for Princess Catherine Dolgoruky to do this? The following day was agreed upon.

The fashionable hour for paying calls in Petersburg was four o'clock, and by this time in the afternoon it was dark throughout the winter, but Society ladies rose late and stayed up until the early hours of morning. Prince Alexis asked the Count if he might take 'Mademoiselle Kira', whom he could hardly address as Kira Vassilievna on so short an acquaintance, for an hour's sleigh ride first, while it was still light. The weather had changed dramatically during Kira's week of confinement. Thick snow had fallen and frosts set in. Sleighs had replaced carriages.

Prince Alexis drove the horses himself, with a servant perched on a step at the back. Kira sat in front beside the Prince, but nets almost touching the ground protected their faces from being hit by snow thrown up from the animals' hooves. Until they got clear of the city they were obliged to limit their speed because of the traffic, and, as Kira had often marvelled, Petersburg had the most varied assortment of people. Some were in sleighs like themselves, and along the Nevsky Prospect rich and poor walked, the rich folk busy shopping.

"Is the Neva frozen yet?" asked Kira.

"The ice is not strong enough to bear any weight. I am sure you are fond of skating?"

"Of course! Who is not?"

"Then perhaps you will allow me the pleasure of escorting you while I am still in Petersburg?"

"Thank you," replied Kira demurely, feeling sure her sister-in-law would say she ought to have a chaperon; but Lydia and Sergei were both away, and if her father approved . . . Aloud she said, "Papa said you spend a great deal of time in Pulkova."

"Yes, I live at the Observatory there. Petersburg has one as well. It is an older institution and has nothing so modern as Pulkova, only there is much interchange of information between the two institutions and I am obliged to

35

spend time at Petersburg now and then."

Conversation ceased because they had got beyond the crowds. Prince Alexis soon had the horses tearing along at a good speed. The bells on the harness jingled cheerfully and Kira felt exhilarated in the crisp air, warm in her furs and with a bearskin covering her knees. She found the sleigh ride particularly pleasurable after being mewed up indoors for several days.

During that time the weather had swiftly changed from autumn to winter. The Winter Palace, the chief imperial residence, was covered with snow, and in this state appeared even longer and more imposing than when its pale blue façade showed bare. Kira had never been inside, only passed the building, and never before had she noticed so many guards on duty. There seemed one in front of every window. She did not know that General Trepov had doubled precautions since the Summer Garden incident, although the Tsar was still in the Crimea.

When the sleigh stopped in front of an entrance, though not the chief one, a guard inspected the pass Alexis carried for Kira, but the Prince was apparently exempt from such a formality. Inside, liveried servants replaced guards. Kira had always heard how enormous the Winter Palace was, but she was not prepared for the numerous corridors with elaborately painted walls and lofty ceiling. They went up a staircase, passed several gilded shut doors, then came to a pair which a servant opened to reveal a new invention she had heard about but not seen. This was a lift. It took them to a higher floor where there was a guard on duty with a servant. However, he bowed respectfully to Prince Alexis and unlocked a large door. Kira inferred this must lead into the private suite of apartments she had heard from Lydia that the Princess Dolgoruky occupied.

There was a hall smelling like a garden in July, for quite a dozen stands were dotted about, and each held a great vase of hothouse flowers. Almost overpowered by the scent, Kira found herself ushered into a comparatively small drawing-room, comfortable and with only a single vase of flowers. A lady was sitting on a sofa.

She looked up as the two entered. Prince Alexis kissed her hand, then presented Kira, who curtsied. It was not her place to speak first, but the Princess, in a soft monotonous voice, at once began to express thanks for her quick courageous action. Kira wanted to correct the adjective courageous and insist that her action had been merely impulsive, but she did not dare. Instead she murmured that she was much obliged "for Your Highness's commendation."

She was invited to take a seat. Only then did she gaze critically at this woman who inspired devotion in a mighty monarch. Tsar Alexander II became guardian to the orphaned and bankrupt family when Catherine Dolgoruky had just reached her teens. She went to school for a few years, then into Society. She was eighteen when the Tsar, many years older, showed his violent love for her. Now she was thirty-two and he was nearly sixty-two. It was an extraordinary situation.

Ash-blond hair contrasted strongly with jet-black eyes. Her figure was slim and tall. She had a pale creamy complexion, a small straight nose, and a very beautiful mouth. Kira had never seen a woman with lips so curved and alluring. Inexperienced in physical love, she could yet understand a man wanting to kiss those lips.

Wine was brought and served. Prince Alexis sat in an armchair, drinking but silent, as if determined to leave conversation to the two ladies. His sister did not linger long on the Summer Garden incident, but turned to a subject of mutual interest, namely that of the Smolny Nobility School at which both had been pupils. The Princess had left many years before Kira entered the establishment. Nothing seemed different. There were the same spartan conditions, occasional 'treats' in the summer of country picnics, then concerts and fêtes in winter, such winter entertainments being attended by parents and distinguished visitors. Rigid rules of behaviour were enforced. No pupil must lean against the back of a chair, or walk quickly.

Kira had hated the school, but she knew it was a privilege to be admitted there, and, as she was told, of great value afterwards in Society. Ladies-in-waiting in the imperial household must be ex-pupils of the Smolny. All the same she wondered if the training had crushed Princess Catherine Dolgoruky's spirit, for Kira was conscious it had crushed her own.

"Did you say you would be returning to Pulkova next week, Alexis?"

"I doubt if I shall have finished my work before the end of November."

Conversation now turned to astronomy. The sister seemed well acquainted with subjects incomprehensible to Kira, like calculated movements of the stars. She let her thoughts wander, wondering what her sister-in-law and her brother would say if they knew of this visit to the woman outlawed by Society. But Papa had sanctioned it, although he had warned her not to inform Lydia and Sergei. That was all very well! Did not Papa realise they were likely to learn about the Summer Garden incident, and so would raise the matter in due course? A serious affair like that attempted assassination would, in the absence of the Tsar, be reported to the Heir Apparent. The latter confided everything in his wife, and through the Tsarevna the story would inevitably reach the ears of a favourite like Lydia.

Kira's musing was interrupted by the entry of the three children and nursemaids. Prince Alexis was obviously a great favourite; and no wonder, when he played games like hide-and-seek with the two eldest. The youngest, who had not been in the Summer Garden, was a mere toddler, scarcely two, but the elder ones rushed towards him and had to be reminded by their mother of their polite duty to the visitor.

George immediately came to her and bowed, announcing, "My name is George, but Papa always calls me Gogo. So do Mama and Uncle Alexis. I am eight years old."

"And I am Olga. I am seven," declared the little girl. She introduced the baby, explaining her name was Catherine.

Kira made a fuss of all three, as she was expected to do. Tea followed. Then Prince Alexis suggested he escorted her home, and the Princess said more thanks before making what amounted to an imperial dismissal. Kira was driven home reflecting that it had been interesting to see the Tsar's mistress, but now the duty of thanks was over, the Princess Dolgoruky would have no wish to see Kira again. Kira only hoped the acquaintance with Prince Alexis would continue.

He fulfilled his promise to take her skating without waiting for the River Neva to become properly frozen. Instead he took her to a lake on the outskirts of Petersburg. The scene was a lively one. The sun was sinking, for daylight ended early in the afternoon, but lanterns and flares provided plenty of light. Prince Alexis linked her arm in his as they stepped out on the ice. Kira was a good skater and could have managed perfectly well by herself, but she found the partnership delightful. Round and round, backwards and forwards, they glided swiftly, and she began to laugh because she was strangely happy. He laughed too.

Warm with exertion, they stopped at last for refreshments, and Kira drank mint tea and nibbled tasty rissoles called *cotletki* which Alexis obtained from one of the many stalls selling food and drink. She was conscious of a surge of delight when he remarked, "This is only the first of our skating afternoons."

Could she be falling in love with him? But that would be absurd when they hardly knew each other. Besides she had hardly met any young men. Lydia had introduced a few to her at the one big function she attended before being summoned to Moscow, and there would be many others her sister-in-law considered eligible.

I am being a silly romantic schoolgirl, Kira told herself. That is all he thinks of me. He likes visiting Papa and talking about astronomy because Papa is so impressed.

Kira had found the conversation between him and his sister about his work very mystifying, and it was the same at home when he was invited to the evening meal. Count Chirnov gave him several invitations because he found the young man interesting, but then he knew a little about astronomy though he had never visited an observatory. Prince Alexis suggested taking the Count to Polkova one day, and he asked Kira if she would like to come too.

"I am sure Kira Vassilievna you would like to look through a telescope and see the planet Jupiter with its moons circling it. That is only possible through a telescope."

In the meantime there were more skatings which Kira enjoyed immensely. He did not worry her with astronomy but asked questions about the other countries where she had lived. Kira happily described all she could remember of that remote land in America and lamented that Russia had sold the colony to the United States.

"How old were you when you left?"

"I was seven, but eight when we finally arrived back here. The journey took a long time because there was no railway east of the Urals, and travelling by sleigh or on horseback necessitated frequent pauses. Roads were almost nonexistent until we reached the Volga.

"Now I look back it astonishes me we never met any gangs of convicts, or saw them marching eastwards. They do

44

have to walk to the places of exile, don't they?"

"Yes, they do. That is why they remain in prison after conviction until spring, starting the journey to Siberia then, but Siberia is a vast country and the convict settlements not that numerous, and they are well scattered."

"So is that Nihilist who tried to kill your sister remaining in prison for the winter? Will he go to Siberia then?"

"That man has been executed," said Prince Alexis. "General Trepov ordered it on his own responsibility. He should really have waited for the Tsar's permission."

"Why didn't he?"

"Possibly he was afraid His Imperial Majesty, who dislikes executions, might have sent the man to Siberia, but Trepov is anxious to wipe out all Nihilists and crush the movement."

"Isn't the Tsar?"

"Naturally, but he tries to be more lenient than his father was. Tsar Nicholas I had a stern temper and anyone thought to be an enemy of the state was doomed. By contrast the present Tsar is a liberal-minded man."

"He must be to liberate the serfs," said Kira. "Do you know him well?"

Alexis smiled. "Well, I and my brothers and sisters are all his wards." He did not refer to the peculiar position one sister occupied and Kira bit her tongue in anger at her tactless question. "His Imperial Majesty is interested in my work in studying the heavens. He occasionally visits Pulkova, as you and your father must do."

Count Chirnov was agreeable for this to take place. He had certainly taken a fancy to Prince Alexis, showed an unexpected enthusiasm for the young man's work, and voiced no objection to the development of a friendship between him and Kira. Already conditioned to marriage some day, but to a husband selected by her dominating sister-in-law, Kira could not help wondering if Papa might not have some idea of that husband being Prince Alexis. The connection with Princess Catherine Dolgoruky would displease Lydia, but no real opposition could be raised if Count Chirnov wished to dispose thus of his daughter.

And would she mind being married to Prince Alexis Michailovich Dolgoruky? As a companion she found him delightful, but asked herself if she could be happy with a man so engrossed in this astronomy of which she was woefully ignorant. He was the first eligible male who seemed real though. The partners at her only ball afterwards paid their respects at Lydia's house, but remained vague insubstantial figures. There would be more. Sergei had spoken of bachelor officers in his regiment.

Time was what she needed, Kira told herself. Time to get used to worldly adult life, as distinct from that depicted in novels secretly circulated among Smolny pupils which laid stress on all-absorbing love. It had existed between the present Tsarina and Tsar Alexander II who had defied his parents until he obtained consent to the marriage. Alas — that love had died long ago, displaced by the Tsar's passion for Princess Catherine Dolgoruky, who lived a cloistered life and was shunned by her relations, except the one brother.

I should not want to make a sacrifice

like that, thought Kira, half-despising herself for coldness. What Mama would have expected from her, and definitely Lydia did, was that she make a socially suitable match, but her father's wishes were a puzzle to Kira. She knew he intended to accept the invitation to Pulkova, and of course she was curious to see the place. To her intense relief, it was arranged sooner than expected, and while Sergei was still on army manoeuvres and Lydia in Moscow. Instinctively she feared that the attentions of Prince Alexis might be viewed unfavourably by her sister-in-law.

A sudden summons from the Observatory Director caused Alexis to return to Pulkova earlier than anticipated, and he duly asked Count Chirnov to accompany him, 'bringing Kira Vassilievna.' They were to stay overnight. The distance from Petersburg was only ten miles, but darkness was necessary for proper viewing of the heavens, so they were to travel one day and return the next.

The Observatory stood on a hill outside the town, and the ascent being gradual, Kira could gaze at the building during their slow approach. It appeared to be divided into three prominent sections, each with a round silver dome kept free of snow through regular sweepings since sections must be slid back for watching the heavens. Additional structures included the Director's residence where she and her father would stay. Alexis also had a suite of rooms there.

The drive leading to the front entrance had been swept clear of snow, and between fir trees was a distant view from the eminence of Petersburg itself, though blurred in the cloudy sky.

"It will clear later," said Alexis.

"Yes, I conclude we need a fine night for observing the sky through your instruments," remarked Count Chirnov.

The entrance was imposing with its classical portico. Word of their arrival had evidently been sent in advance, since waiting to receive the guests was the Director, Herr Struve, a Dane and son of the first man to hold this office. The Pulkova Observatory had only been in existence for forty years.

After being shown their bedchambers, Kira and her father were conducted by a servant to a small salon. Here tea and cakes were served to them, the Director, and Prince Alexis. Herr Struve explained that work at Pulkova was mainly concerned with mapping of stars and compiling records of their movements in the sky.

"We do very little with the planetary system."

By this Kira gathered he meant the planets, the sun, and the moon. She looked questioningly at Prince Alexis who reassured her.

"Yes, I promised you should see the planet Jupiter and its moons, only no viewing is possible until the weather improves." It was snowing outside now. "The snow won't last, so later tonight you shall look through our big telescope at the giant planet."

Tea being finished there came a tour of the Observatory. Kira had not been prepared for such furnishing starkness — just stiff-backed chairs and a few tables. They were provided to be of use to astronomers hard at work. It was instruments that were of prime importance and they dominated the scene. Kira was impressed by the iron staircases leading up and down, also the railed galleries built as high as the window tops around the walls in some rooms.

One of these was a library where the Director proudly showed a precious possession: the manuscripts of Johann Kepler. Papa knew who the writer was, but Kira did not and she was grateful to Prince Alexis who quietly explained he was a famous German astronomer. He had lived in the latter half of the sixteenth century and beginning of the seventeenth.

On one wall in the library hung a portrait of Tsar Nicholas I who had been responsible for erecting the Observatory on what was then an imperial estate. It had cost over two hundred thousand pounds and the Tsar intended it to be the foremost astronomical centre in the world, even superior to Greenwich in England. Pulkova had the biggest telescope and when they reached the room where that instrument was placed Alexis promised Kira to bring her back when it was dark. The snow was stopping, as he had foretold.

51

Her wish was fulfilled. They all returned late in the evening and she watched Alexis swing the instrument into position, for it lay in a kind of loose cradle. He directed her eye to the eyepiece and at once she picked out one round little object. It was a globe and had tiny globes moving round it.

Kira could not help shrieking with excitement, then recollected she was not behaving as a young lady should. She stood aside for her father to view.

She saw that by the enthusiastic way Alexis talked about the skies and showed her other celestial objects of special interest that he was not worried by the cold. Kira began to wonder what effect constant study of the heavens had upon a man. Surely human beings must seem petty by comparison. Yet Alexis could enjoy games with Gogo and Olga, and skating with her, but would marriage appeal to him as it did to ordinary men? He was so devoted to astronomy.

I should be foolish to lose my heart to him, thought Kira.

3

A FEW days after the exciting Pulkova visit, Kira received a letter from Lydia, saying her Aunt Mavra was much better so she should be returning to Petersburg the following week. Sergei's military manoeuvres would soon be over and he too would be back. "Then we shall resume normal life and I shall really start the task of launching you."

Lydia writes as if I were a ship, thought Kira, smiling to herself. The next paragraph was a homily on the necessity of behaving in lively fashion and seriously encouraging attention from the suitable *partis* to whom her sister-in-law would introduce her.

"Do bear in mind that no male is attracted by a stiff dummy, and candidly, my dear, that is the impression you gave at the Arkady ball. You complain of shyness but that you must overcome."

Kira folded up the sheet and sighed.

She had not felt a stiff dummy with Prince Alexis, and now she was missing his frequent calls at the house, listening to learned astronomical talk between him and Papa although she understood very little of it, and above all enjoying skating with him. The prospect of society-girl-husband-pursuit to which Lydia would soon be subjecting her was most unwelcome.

Two days later came an unexpected visitor in the shape of her brother Sergei. The manoeuvres must have ended earlier than she thought, and when told Kira eagerly ran downstairs to the library where she knew he would be with Count Chirnov. From childhood Kira had adored Sergei. He was a boy of fourteen when she was taken to Russian America, and she had cried bitterly at their parting. Her mother had scolded her for lack of self-control, saying, "Do you not think Papa and I will miss your brother, but his career must come first."

Reunion after a lapse of years; Kira looked with awe at the good-looking young man in the striking Preobrajenski uniform, his laughing face turned to her as he jokingly remarked that his little sister had changed from being a baby to a young lady — oh, a very young lady, but he should not insult her by calling her a child. This won the eight-year Kira's heart in spite of being aware she had a long time to go before reaching that stage in her life. After this she worshipped Sergei more intensely than ever, blind to faults that even his parents noticed.

Count Chirnov reproved him for extravagance and gambling. He settled Sergei's present accumulation of debts but warned him he should get nothing further and must certainly turn over a new leaf when he married. Both Count and Countess agreed to his betrothal and marriage to Princess Lydia, sister of Sergei's friend, Prince Ivan Granovski. The family was an illustrious one, and they had been impressed by Sergei, when he wrote of friendship with Prince Ivan. This friend died of smallpox shortly after his sister's marriage which took place in splendid style. The betrothal had been short because Sergei had won Lydia's approval long before, only there could be nothing official without parental consent and the Count and Countess were then on the long journey westwards.

Kira did her utmost to become fond of her sister-in-law, but found it impossible because Lydia showed little affection for her. She was not that kind of person, and if she had been present today, Kira would have repressed her extreme joy at seeing Sergei again, and not rushed up to him expecting a fond embrace. He broke off the conversation with their father to greet her, but Sergei was as serious as if he were on parade. Turning to the Count, Kira saw his expression was one of shocked horror.

"What has happened?" she enquired.

"The Tsar was nearly blown up by a Nihilist bomb on the train journey from the Crimea to Moscow. Oh, it was known he intended to visit Moscow, but the date was kept as secret as possible because of warnings from Petersburg issued by General Trepov himself. There has been trouble here with some incident in the Summer Garden."

"We know about that," interrupted the Count. "Continue your story, Sergei."

"Those Nihilists found out, but they timed the bomb for the wrong train. You see there are always two imperial specials, the Tsar using the second one, but for some reason he travelled in the first train and this left earlier than planned."

"Is His Imperial Majesty unhurt?"

Sergei nodded reassuringly, then explained details. Some of the plotters installed themselves in a house near the Kursky Station and managed to construct a tunnel right underneath the platform where trains from the South drew in. Here they planted a time bomb, but with confusion over the Tsar's trains it exploded after Alexander's arrival.

Kira was as shocked as her father to hear of this near-tragedy. It horrified her that the Nihilists had planned such a deadly operation. She felt pride in how she had saved the Princess Dolgoruky from one, yet was nervous of the incident being related to Sergei and perhaps him learning about Pulkova. Sergei told his wife everything and she did not want Lydia to know about the friendship with Prince Alexis, nor the visit to the Winter Palace.

However, Sergei, with due apologies to his father, said he must leave at once to keep an appointment. According to him this was with the colonel of his regiment but actually it was with a brother officer and they had arranged to have a game of faro. He had returned to Petersburg only that morning, and made it clear he visited Count Chirnov at the earliest opportunity.

"Lydia will be back tomorrow," he added. "She is being accompanied by a cousin, Count Matvejevi. He is not a Granovski, but related on her mother's side."

"Shall I meet her at the railway station?"

"Yes, she will expect it, and she is anxious to introduce you to this relative."

"She did not mention him in the letter I received two days ago," said Kira. "In that she said she was not coming back until next week."

"She has altered her plans. There was a letter waiting for me at home."

With that Sergei made his farewells and departed. He was first obliged to visit a money lender, although of course he did not say so, for his father disapproved of reckless gambling and would be furious to know his son was in such straits. He had come to Sergei's rescue before his marriage but imagined he was behaving differently now. Poor Kira would have been broken-hearted had she known the difference between her idealised portrait of this brother and his real self. Sergei was hoping she would marry the Count Matvejevi, an extremely wealthy widower, only just returned from years in Finland, so Lydia had told him in the letter which arrived in Petersburg this morning. Lydia, knowing the state of their finances, was triumphantly bringing the Count for that purpose and delighted he was willing to come at short notice. The sick aunt had raised no objection to the two leaving. She had secretly been told what her niece hoped to achieve, and agreed a second wife of aristocratic birth would be just the thing for Hippolyte.

Prince Granovski, Lydia's father, had married beneath him. His wife's family was connected with trade, a fact concealed in Petersburg. Even Count Chirnov was ignorant of that, and he and the Countess had been so proud of their son marrying a Granovski, while trade was despised in their echelon of Society. Hippolyte Karlovich Matvejevi, widowed last spring, had made enough money in Finland to retire, by bribery obtain a title, and came to Moscow ostensibly to see his Aunt Mavra, but really to persuade his Cousin Lydia to introduce him to her aristocratic circle and possibly to find him a suitable bride.

Kira dutifully went to meet Lydia and the guest the latter was bringing. The station looked as usual, whereas she expected it to be bristling with guards until the Tsar was back and in the Winter Palace, but he was still in Moscow. Count Chirnov had remarked on that the previous evening as father and daughter sat alone in the drawing-room.

"I called on General Trepov and he gave me that information. When His Imperial Majesty returns I anticipate a summons from him. He will want to give me instructions regarding the Bulgarian affair."

Kira knew it was no use saying she wished she could go too. Her father had already turned down that request. It cheered her a little to hear him repeat that he did not think he should be sent until March, for on March the second were to take place celebrations of the twenty-five years Tsar Alexander II had reigned.

"General Trepov told me Prince Alexander of Bulgaria, as well as his uncle the Grand Duke of Hesse-Darmstadt, will be attending them."

Considering one was the Tsarina Marie's nephew and the other her brother, that was to be expected, also the return from abroad of the sickly Tsarina herself.

"I spoke with the General about your part in the Summer Garden incident," went on Count Chirnov. "He had been compelled to report a Nihilist attempt on the Princess Dolgoruky's life to the Tsarevich, but His Imperial Highness received it without comment."

No wonder, thought Kira, aware of the hatred borne by the Heir Apparent against his father's mistress.

"As there was no enquiry concerning the person who deflected the assassin's bullet, General Trepov did not mention your name. I asked him to keep silent about you, and your visit to the Winter Palace, unless pressed, which is now very unlikely. Once the Tsarevich was satisfied the Nihilist had been given the death penalty, he showed no further interest. Of course when the Tsar returns it will be different. I know he will congratulate me on having such a brave and quick-to-act daughter."

Greatly relieved that neither Sergei nor Lydia was likely to hear about her involvement, Kira went next day to the railway station. She found she had several minutes to wait for the train's arrival, so walked up and down the platform because, in spite of her warm furs, she found it too cold to stand still. Oblivious to the bustle of porters, passengers, and people like herself meeting friends, her thoughts strayed to Prince Alexis. Again she tried to puzzle out the enigma of this dual-sided young man. He was pleasant and courteous like any other young aristocrat, yet in her eyes infinitely superior. He was also the astronomer. The short time spent at Pulkova had left its mark on Kira. How could a man regularly contemplate the phenomena of the heavens, the infinity of space as shown by the multitude of stars, but still partake of ordinary life? No wonder he shunned his contemporaries, with the exception of his lonely sister, and preferred to be in an austere observatory room carrying out the study he loved, concerned with matters far beyond Petersburg, mighty Russia, the planet Earth, as he devoted hours to studying the stars, great suns far removed from our own solar system . . .

Kira was suddenly jolted back to the platform which the train was rapidly approaching. It arrived. It stopped and the engine emitted clouds of smoke, obscuring the crowds. Then it cleared and she saw Sergei's wife.

"My dear sister!" Lydia's greeting sounded to Kira as chilly as the ice covering the River Neva. "This is Count Matvejevi. Hippolyte, this is Kira Vassilievna."

Kira was not greatly taken with Lydia's cousin. He was a man of medium height with small blue eyes, small mouth, thickset neck, and her first impression was that he looked extremely pleased with himself. Age? Certainly he was some years older than either Sergei or Prince Alexis.

Porters attended to the baggage and the three walked out of the station to where a conveyance awaited them. Naturally Lydia talked about the Nihilist attempt to kill Tsar Alexander II.

"I heard it was by pure chance he travelled on the first train. That is supposed to ensure the safety of the track, but the engine of the second had developed a slight defect and His Majesty refused to wait for this to be remedied so reached Moscow well in advance of the time he was expected. I believe he was actually entering the Kremlin when there was a terrific explosion at the Kursky Railway Station."

"How did you know about it?"

"When it happened. My aunt's house is not far away. Everything swayed, ornaments fell down and pictures dropped from the walls. We thought there was an earthquake. Hippolyte was walking in the street outside, coming to call, and he says people flung themselves upon the ground."

After arrival at Sergei's house, Kira accompanied her sister-in-law to her bedchamber, 'to help me unpack', which was absurd. The two women sat on a couch while the personal maid bustled around performing that task, and she might have been as devoid of hearing as the furniture for Lydia spoke without restraint.

"I realise your life must have been tiresomely dull while alone with Papa in Petersburg."

"No, I have enjoyed the quiet," replied Kira, then knew she had been tactless.

"Quiet indeed! Really, Kira, you are the most stupid, unambitious girl in the world. You are saying that while I was in Moscow you were content to lead a humdrum existence, shopping, walking, reading, and I suppose entertaining Papa with your piano-playing that sent him to sleep. With all respect to my esteemed father-in-law, I have found him a dull man, and it is clear you take after him. Thank God, Sergei is different. He cannot exist without card-playing and racing and other masculine excitements."

Though Kira was unaware, the last-named included flirtations with women of easy virtue not in Society, and were the cause of private quarrels between him and his wife; he arguing 'everyone' was the same.

"Not the Tsarevich!"

He was indeed a model of conjugal fidelity. Sergei acknowledged this; then added, what about the Tsar?

"If you brought a Dolgoruky female into this house I should leave you on the spot."

Not that Lydia believed Sergei, on whom she doted, would behave like the Tsar. Moreover she knew her friends' husbands had affairs with stage women and others of that kind, but they behaved discreetly and there was no insult to the wife as had been inflicted on the Tsarina Marie. However, Lydia wished devoutly that Sergei was not so reckless with money. She had brought him a very large dowry, yet he was always borrowing from her and never repaying the debt. How much her fortune had decreased she did not know, but she felt it to be important that Hippolyte — the wealthy Hippolyte, married Kira. Then he might help, she hoped.

Nagged by Lydia, Kira endeavoured to be pleasant to Hippolyte but he roused no affection in her, and one should have that, although not love, for one's partner in marriage. Besides, as a companion she found him very dull, especially when she compared him with Prince Alexis.

"Hippolyte is looking for a second wife as soon as his period of mourning for the first is over. Now it is up to you, Kira, to fix him. If you do not, some other girl will. The first marriage did not last long enough for any children to be born, so there are no encumbrances. I trust you are not cherishing foolish schoolgirl notions of romantic love. An aristocrat marries for — well, suitability as the prime consideration. She may love in addition, as I did with your brother. You can soon make yourself very fond of Hippolyte if you think along sensible lines."

Never, thought Kira. She snubbed Hippolyte as openly as she dare, but he was too conceited to be snubbed easily. With what he regarded as great wit, he called her Ice Maiden. Lydia scolded her, and even Sergei took her to task.

"But I don't care for him," retorted Kira. "You married for love. Why shouldn't I?"

This silenced Sergei; who had married Lydia first for her fortune, secondly for her family's high position in Society, but he had never felt love. They jogged along happily and he was quite aware of her devotion to him. Perhaps he could bring pressure to bear on Kira when Papa had gone to Bulgaria, he told Lydia.

"Papa indulges her so ridiculously. If she tells him we want her to marry Hippolyte and she does not want to do so, he will take her side and spoil everything for us."

"Hippolyte will have got tired of Kira's frigid behaviour long before your father goes to Bulgaria. Oh, she is a most unnatural girl! She is hopeless with other men."

The more Kira saw of Lydia's choice of possible suitors, especially Hippolyte, the more she became convinced of Prince

Alexis's superiority.

I could love him, she decided. Then followed the sad conviction that he was too absorbed in astronomy to bother seriously with marriage.

She hoped her father might hear something about him when summoned by the Tsar for briefing regarding Bulgaria. Alexander did refer to Kira's action in the Summer Garden, but he deemed it sufficient to send a message of thanks through the Count. Kira did not expect, or wish for, a second visit to the Winter Palace.

She went several times to the Anitchkov Palace, residence of the Tsarevich and Tsarevna, since Lydia and Sergei were great favourites of that illustrious couple. Followers of the future Tsar were called the Anitchkov Palace set and they dominated Petersburg Society, which lacked any lead from the Winter Palace. The ailing Tsarina was either abroad or unable to be present at functions. The Tsar spent his leisure hours in the seclusion of Princess Catherine Dolgoruky's private apartments, seldom performing social duties.

The Tsarevna, the Heir's wife, was a Danish princess, and had been betrothed to Tsar Alexander II's eldest son who died, bequeathing his fiancée to the next in line of succession, his brother the Grand Duke Alexander, now Tsarevich. As Grand Duke Nicholas lay dying, he had placed Princess Dagmar's hand in that of Alexander, imploring the two to marry.

"You, my dear bride, your destiny will still be accomplished; you will be Tsarina of Russia one day. Marry my brother. He is as true as crystal."

The ambitious Danish princess very properly took a year to consider the matter, then consented. The new Heir to the Russian throne was, and it was believed had always been, in love with her. She was beautiful and charming, and they were an extremely happy couple. She bore him five children, and although she made a pretence of never meddling in politics, it was well known he confided to her any state secrets he knew and asked her advice. She prevented him from expressing openly his disagreement with most of the Tsar's policies. In spite of this, there was veiled discord between the two men. Regarding her mother-in-law, the Tsarina Marie, the Tsarevna joined her husband in hating Princess Dolgoruky, but nobody dared criticise the Tsar to his face.

A son more unlike the father could hardly be imagined, mentally and physically. The Tsarevich was a giant of a man who possessed extraordinary physical strength. For example, he could break in two a silver plate with his hands. He lacked the diplomatic ability of the Tsar. In fact, the time when he must succeed to the throne was dreaded by statesmen and reformers.

He disliked entertaining while his wife loved it. She had a passion for dancing, as well as for dress, and nothing pleased her more than to be hostess at a reception-cum-ball in the Anitchkov Palace. During such functions the Tsarevich would not permit a word of German to be spoken, and even fined guests who used that language. He permitted French, since it was the Court language, but Russian must have priority. He supported a Panslavonic movement which pressed use of the native tongue and culture. This was another cause of bad feeling between Tsar and Tsarevich. The former was international in outlook, desiring Russia to become a force in European affairs, not a country isolating itself from them.

The Tsarevich's attitude was remarkable because his mother was German, and he loved her dearly; but his wife was a Danish princess and there was intense bitterness in Denmark against Prussia who had deprived Denmark of two duchies, Schleswig and Holstein. The Tsarevna's anti-German prejudice prevailed.

There was to be a reception with dancing at the Anitchkov Palace on the Feast of Epiphany, and as the Tsar had signified his intention of being present, prospective guests wondered if he would indulge in his usual joking pastime of speaking German, thus infuriating his heir, who could not presume to fine him. Kira heard the conjectures among ladies who came to gossip in Lydia's drawing-room.

Her father was confined to bed with

a chill, so was unable to attend the reception and also the outdoor ritual Blessing of the Waters which took place on the morning of the Epiphany Feast. Kira went with Lydia. Sergei was with his regiment.

Superstition had originated this ritual act, now one carried out by the Russian Orthodox Church. In Petersburg the waters were those of the frozen River Neva, and before dawn on the cold January morning the city was thronged with people. Lydia and Kira, attended by Hippolyte, had reserved places near the Winter Palace, from where they had an excellent view of the colourful procession as it emerged from what was called the Jordan Door and marched to that place on the Neva where a hole was already cut in the ice.

The procession was headed by a priest swinging a censer, followed by another carrying a cross, then more clergy, then choir boys of the Palace Cathedral. The clergy wore heavy gold vestments. The choir boys were in scarlet uniforms and sang a hymn as they walked. Next came persons of importance, such as ministers of state and foreign ambassadors. The Tsar, in Cossack uniform, came last.

The actual ceremony did not take long. It was daylight now but bitterly cold, and the hole that had been cut for water would be frozen over before the end of the day. The archbishop conjured the Devil from his retreat, salt was cast, the cross dipped, water sprinkled over the Tsar who uttered a quick blessing, then waited while selected priests drew up bucketfuls for church use. After that he returned to the Palace and it was left for humble folk to press forward filling bottles with the water, now believed to possess healing powers until ice covered it again.

Hippolyte, grumbling about the intense cold declared he was thankful the ceremony was over. Petersburg was colder than Helsingfors — the Finnish town where he had lived for many years. He held an arm of each lady in his charge, pushing a way to their waiting sleigh; and it was while he was assisting Lydia to take a seat, Kira, standing by, saw Prince Alexis Dolgoruky passing. She expected a greeting and was ready to acknowledge it, but he disappeared in the crowd without seeing her. Well, she knew he was in Petersburg, and decided he must have been sent, as he often was, to take notes of observations from Pulkova to the capital's smaller observatory. If only he would call on Papa!

Kira ventured into her father's bedchamber before leaving for the Anitchkov Palace reception, saying apologetically that she thought he might like to see her new evening gown. The Count complimented her, showing less enthusiasm than he actually felt, for Kira made a charming picture in pale pink velvet trimmed with creamy lace round neck, shoulders, and skirt flounces, while her dark curls were threaded with pearls and pink satin ribbons.

But he did say, "I shall be sorry to leave you, child, when I go to Bulgaria. I forgot to tell you because I developed this chill, but just before that the Tsar spoke about you, regretting he had not found an opportunity of thanking you in person for the service you rendered Princess Dolgoruky. He hoped he should have a chance to do so at the Anitchkov reception. So you had better be prepared for this honour tonight."

"Oh, Papa, surely not!"

Kira was conscious of colour flooding her cheeks. They were burning at the awful possibility of such thanks, not because she minded being singled out by the Tsar, but because other people like the Tsarevich and Tsarevna would overhear. Everyone would know about the Summer Garden and her saving Princess Dolgoruky's life! She had thought her father wanted to keep the episode from Sergei and Lydia. He had spoken to General Trepov . . .

As if reading her thoughts, Count Chirnov said, "I am afraid you cannot stop the Tsar, child. Anyway, Lydia cannot interfere with you while I am in Bulgaria."

"She will, Papa."

"You are not going to live with Sergei. The Tsar proposes to honour you by appointing you as an extra Maid of Honour to the Tsarina. She is returning soon, in plenty of time for the Jubilee Celebrations, although the doctors advise her to remain in Cannes until mid-April."

The Tsarina suffered with her chest and Kira had heard it said she was consumptive. Kira remembered imperial visits to the Smolny and knew her to be a gentle, kind person, who would do anything to please her husband. What he ordered she would carry out, even to the extent of having in her household a girl who had saved her husband's mistress from an assassin's bullet.

Attendance on a sick woman might be trying, but Kira was thankful for this chance of escape from long residence in the home of Sergei and Lydia. She kissed her father, then went to their house where she was to meet them before they all set out for the Anitchkov Palace.

On arrival, visitors were relieved of cloaks and shawls by footmen in red and gold livery, then moved forward to ascend the curving marble staircase, where, on the landing above, stood the host and hostess waiting to receive their guests. Kira's heart swelled with pride at the handsome figure her brother presented in his Preobrajenski uniform. Her father had recently annoyed her by saying Sergei was putting on weight, but she considered it added to his dignity. Lydia looked elegant in green satin and her Granovski family emeralds. She had the air and bearing of an aristocrat which her cousin on the maternal side, Hippolyte, could never achieve.

The three walked slowly upward under the brilliant light spread from crystal chandeliers, and the two ladies made their curtsies to the Imperial couple. The bulky, gigantic Tsarevich always made Kira think of a great bear. He never smiled on formal occasions and his manner of receiving guests was abrupt to the point of being uncouth. By contrast, the small dainty Tsarevna exuded charm.

Guests next passed into the ballroom. Here people were standing in groups, chatting as they waited for the Tsar to arrive. Not until then could dancing begin. Thinking of the ordeal ahead that Papa had warned her about, Kira found this interval made her more apprehensive than ever. She was annoyed too by Hippolyte's possessive attitude and his declaration that he intended to dance with her most of the evening.

"I don't think that would be proper," said Kira.

She felt her cheek tapped playfully, but with underlying purpose, by Lydia's fan.

"As Hippolyte is in a way your relative, such conventions do not apply."

"The relationship is with you, not me."

Lydia paid no attention to this retort. She sauntered off to join a group of friends, and as Sergei had already vanished, Kira was left alone with Hippolyte and forced to listen to his banter.

"I have heard about the strict regime in the Smolny School, and indeed you cannot forget its teachings, can you, Kira Vassilievna? We must see what can be done. You must put yourself in my hands and let me be the devoted tutor."

Kira proposed they joined Lydia's group.

"Coy at being alone with me, aren't you?"

"Don't be ridiculous."

"Ah, but I am serious about you, Kira Vassilievna. Cannot you see I am forming the hope of being accepted as your husband once I am free to make the offer?"

By being free, he meant when his year of widowhood ended, and Kira neither wanted any offer, nor did she mean to accept one. She did not mind other girls ogling him, encouraged by their mothers.

At this moment the arrival of the Tsar was announced by a major-domo and, as if by magic, the entire company formed itself into a semi-circle, men bowing and women curtseying. The exalted Majesty of Russia entered the ballroom, followed by Tsarevich and Tsarevna. Behind them were two gentlemen-in-waiting, one wearing uniform and the other civilian evening dress.

In spite of being in his sixty-second year, Alexander II held his tall figure erect, and though his hair was beginning to turn grey it was quite plentiful. He had rather singular sparkling blue eyes, which were immediately perceived by Kira. He paused in front of her, addressing her by her two first names, just as he used to do when visiting the Smolny. Rising, she was obliged to move a couple of paces forward, whereas Hippolyte, like the rest of the company, remained motionless. How curiously familiar, somehow, was the Tsar's face, she thought. Yet it was quite three years since she had seen him on his visit to the Smolny during her schooling there.

The Tsar was addressing her in German, a language used with obvious intent to annoy his son, but Kira fortunately was as fluent in that as in French and Russian.

"Your name has recently come to our notice as saving one of our subjects from an assassin's attack in the Summer Garden. We give you our personal thanks, Kira Vassilievna."

She could sense astonishment oozing from Tsarevich and Tsarevna. The Tsar was smiling, and his smile had a mischievous element. He showed he was enjoying disobeying the rule of the Anitchkov Palace regarding the use of German.

He said, "Are you still levying a fine on any guest who speaks your own mother's language here, Sasha? Well, one of our aides will settle the debt. Alexis Michailovich, pay His Imperial Highness the forfeit he exacts from us."

Yes, the second aide-de-camp, the one not in military uniform, was Prince Alexis Dolgoruky!

Before continuing his progress along the ballroom, the Tsar turned again to Kira. She felt the Tsarevna was listening avidly.

"Your father, our old friend Count Chirnov, told us of the acquaintance with Prince Alexis Dolgoruky after the Summer Garden incident, and how he showed you both around Pulkova Observatory. Are you intending to become a female astronomer?"

Those eyes! Why, they were exactly like Alexis's!

Recollecting herself, Kira replied, "I fear I am not clever enough to cherish such an ambition, Your Majesty. But I did enjoy seeing the wonderful work carried on at Pulkova."

"You must discuss it with Prince Alexis then. He has our permission to partner you in the polonaise."

This was always the first dance at

any Court ball. Having circled the line of guests, addressing a few specially favoured, Tsar Alexander, as etiquette demanded, started to dance with the Tsarevna, she being the lady of highest rank present. Following them came the Tsarevich with an elderly Grand Duchess, his aunt. Then Kira found herself led on the floor by Prince Alexis.

4

BY starting the evening's dancing with the polonaise, the reception at the Anitchkov was following an established custom in force at the Winter Palace until social functions had been suspended during the last year or so, presumably due to the Tsarina Marie's ill-health.

In that establishment the opening polonaise was akin to a stately walk, when couples in order of rank proceeded from one enormous hall to another, but here only the ballroom was circled. Usually the Tsar and Tsarina took no further part in the succession of quadrilles, waltzes, cotillions, and mazurkas that followed. They sat on the thrones and conversed with guests singled out for attention, then retired after supper. But tonight Tsar Alexander left before the serving of that meal and his two aides were obliged to accompany him. He had behaved towards his heir in a particularly aggravating manner, speaking constantly in German because he knew the irritation it caused. The Tsarevich looked more than ever like a raging bear when the Tsar departed and he was able to relax from a rigid facial expression.

Until this departure Prince Alexis remained with Kira, causing her completely to disregard what she had said to Hippolyte about convention. She now cared nothing about other people's observations on her conduct. Her one idea was to avoid Lydia and Sergei and to enjoy the company of Alexis without their interference. If only her father had been present, everything would have been simple. He liked the Prince and would have approved the attention she permitted him to bestow upon her.

Once the polonaise was over, Kira really expected Alexis to leave her after a few minutes' chat. There had been no opportunity for conversation during that dignified dance, but now he steered her towards a corner, then realised they were standing near one of the enormous porcelain stoves that heated the room; and, by the time they moved away from it, they were hemmed in by men in uniform and females in billowing tulle skirts. He managed to enquire how she had enjoyed the festivities of Christmas when the orchestra struck up music for a quadrille, and Kira thought that would be the signal for him to bow and leave her. Instead he led her to form a set begun by three couples — people unknown to her and to him.

She was still with Alexis during the interval after the dance and this provided her with an opportunity to remark on her surprise at seeing him in Petersburg so early in the month.

"When I last met you at Pulkova you said you should not be coming here until the end of January. How is your astronomical research proceeding?"

Alexis explained a summons from the Tsar caused him to leave Pulkova yesterday.

"I think I told you how interested His Imperial Majesty is in astronomy. Sometimes he pays a private visit to the Observatory, but he is fully occupied with state affairs just now, so wanted a report from me. We spent a stimulating evening

86

together, and shall continue discussions after leaving the Anitchkov tonight."

He was certainly a favourite with the Tsar, and a favourite granted privileges. There was a joint interest in astronomy, his relationship to Princess Catherine Dolgoruky, and he too had been an imperial ward. Maybe there was a link stronger than those three, thought Kira, who was beginning to wonder if that marked likeness about the eyes betrayed close kinship. Prince Alexis might be the product of one of His Majesty's earlier liaisons and adopted by the late Prince Dolgoruky at Imperial request — no, command! She had heard of that practice among members of the aristocracy, so a Romanoff might follow it as well.

Kira was also curious about Alexis's presence this evening, for he could not be an officially appointed aide-de-camp. Impossible to ask such a question, but Alexis, unprompted, supplied the explanation. He was closeted with the Tsar when the latter's chief valet reported that the aide due to attend had been taken ill after the Blessing of the Waters and was now in bed delirious with fever.

"So I was ordered to attend in his place, in spite of my not being able to appear in military uniform. Of course His Majesty has other aides-de-camp and one of these could have been summoned, but it amuses him to shock the Tsarevich and he picked on me as a means of doing so. The Tsarevich hates all Dolgorukys. Then it was rather a slight to appear with one aide-de-camp in uniform and the other in civilian garb. The Tsar has a peculiar sense of humour at times."

"Still, His Imperial Highness the Tsarevich could not criticise any action of his father the Tsar."

★ ★ ★

They were chatting between dances. After the quadrille she had remained with him. Now the orchestra was starting again, and this time it was an alluring waltz. In the waltz one danced as an isolated couple, not part of a set.

He did not ask her to be his partner, although it was very incorrect to have three dances running with a lady. Alexis just took her acquiescence for granted and led her on to the floor, getting away before Lydia, who was advancing in their direction, reached them. Kira felt one hand of the Prince pressed lightly against her back, while the other clasped one of hers firmly. She held her skirt with the free one. He kept his body the correct distance of twelve inches away from hers, yet she felt very close to him, nearer than she had been since he supported her after injury in the Summer Garden, and certainly when he took her arm as they skated.

The swirling waltz music transported Kira into paradise, a world in which she was under the spell of a powerful enchanter. Her will seemed completely dominated by Alexis, and in spite of the space between them, she was acutely conscious of his masculinity. She wished the magical dance could go on for ever.

But the music stopped and, still in a dreamlike state, she walked off the floor with him, unconcerned at critical glances from other guests, but straightway she came up against reality. Intercepting their progress was Sergei. There was a look on her brother's face that Kira had never seen before. It was compounded of anger and hatred.

Instinctively she blamed Lydia, who, furious at Kira's disregard of convention, must have sent Sergei to intervene. But there was more than that. Her brother stood and spoke as if he were dealing with an enemy, and though his attitude was aggressive, she sensed an element of fear, which was extraordinary, for she had always looked upon him as a courageous soldier. He would never flinch from enemy fire, believed Kira. He did not submit to Lydia's bossing because he was afraid of his wife but through adoration of her. Count Chirnov invoked timidity in him, but fathers did. She, Kira, loved Papa, yet she held him in awe, as must Sergei . . .

"How dare you presume to dance with my sister, Prince Alexis Dolgoruky, once an officer in the Preobrajenski?"

Kira stared in bewilderment at the two men facing each other. Lydia rushed up, storming at Prince Alexis.

The way she hissed reminded Kira of encountering a snake when gathering berries in the country last summer, and had she not been accompanied by a servant with a gun, the reptile would have attacked her since it was in a startled rage. To move backwards would incite it so Kira stood still, thankful when old Fyodor ended the danger by firing, but — yes, in this palace ballroom — she had a vision of malevolent eyes and forked tongue darting in and out of the snake's mouth.

Of course Lydia was furious because she had deserted Hippolyte and given three dances in succession to another man, a very improper course of conduct. Kira had expected her sister-in-law to be angry, but was disgusted she should behave in so undignified a fashion. It was strange she should address Prince Alexis as if she knew him. Kira had not been aware of that.

People around were staring, conscious of a quarrel, showing curiosity but trying to conceal their interest. The Prince remained unruffled.

He said to Sergei, "His Imperial Majesty commanded me to dance with your sister, Captain Chirnov."

"For the polonaise, and that was an

amazing whim! But dance after dance! You had not been previously introduced to my sister, and you never would have been as far as I was concerned."

"Ah, but I had, and Count Chirnov raised no objection to my taking her skating, nor would he have been annoyed that I have been partnering her in the waltz."

Here Lydia intervened, "I have just learnt from the Tsarevna that before her the Tsar, when speaking to Kira, referred to some incident in the Summer Garden and a visit to Pulkova. It looks as if there has been a considerable degree of acquaintance while we have been away, Sergei." And wheeling round she said to Kira, "You have been very deceitful. As for your father, I cannot understand him."

Looking at Prince Alexis, Kira saw a smile lurking round his lips.

"I did not enlighten the Count about my previous acquaintance with you and your husband, Princess Lydia."

"You sought out my father on purpose to annoy me by obtaining an introduction to my young sister," accused Sergei.

"What an extraordinary idea!" There was a scornful note in Prince Alexis's voice which astonished Kira. Then he began a brief explanation. "I was in the Summer Gardens when your sister saved Princess Catherine Dolgoruky from a Nihilist bullet. I escorted her home, was graciously received by your father and the hospitality of his house was extended to me. As for previous dealings between you and me in the Preobrajenski more than ten years ago, I saw no reason to mention them. The Count knows nothing about that special little matter, I take it?"

"Little matter!" snorted Lydia.

She might have said a great deal more, but there was a loud announcement, "His Imperial Majesty is retiring for the night." At once the assembly was frozen into immobility, except the host and hostess who had the duty of accompanying the monarch and his attendants to the front door. Alexis bowed to Kira. With the other aide-de-camp he then followed the Tsar, Tsarevich, and Tsarevna.

"We three will leave as soon as I can obtain His Imperial Highness's permission," said Sergei to Lydia.

"But Hippolyte — where is he?"

"Call a servant to find him, and tell him to stay until the end. Now I must go to the front hall and speak to the Tsarevich when he is at liberty."

Sergei melted into the crowd and Kira was left to endure more scolding from Lydia. Nobody else came near. Everyone seemed waiting for the return of the imperial host when dancing would be continued.

"Hippolyte was disgusted with you. When you danced the quadrille with that creature, he came to me and said he should ask Countess Bukaty." The lady Lydia referred to was a dashing young widow. "I never thought you would waltz as well with Prince Alexis, and I am sure Hippolyte did not because he again approached me, only there was such a crush I could not get close enough to stop you going on the floor. How could you be such a fool! Well, the Countess Bukaty will grab Hippolyte now. As for your reputation!"

"Papa approves of Prince Alexis."

"He doesn't know the truth about him."

"What truth?"

"Never mind! Oh, Hippolyte, this silly girl is ready to dance with you now, but Sergei is so angry he is sweeping us off home. Don't let us drag you away, though."

"You look very upset, my dear Lydia, but I am sure Kira Vassilievna acted against her sense of propriety when she danced three times with Prince Dolgoruky."

"Oh, she does, and she regrets it very much now."

But Kira ignored the hint to make her apologies to Hippolyte and he, piqued by her indifference, began to talk about the amiability of Countess Bukaty.

"I must hasten to her side before dancing commences again. She has promised to be my partner in the cotillion."

With a couple of triumphant bows he departed, leaving Lydia to vent her anger on Kira.

"You see, you'll be a wallflower for the rest of the season. Men will be afraid to ask a young lady who has made herself so conspicuous by dancing three times with the same partner and looking like you did in that waltz. How could you disgrace me and Sergei so? And with Alexis Dolgoruky of all men!"

"Why are you so prejudiced against him?" enquired Kira.

She received no answer because the entire company stood to attention as the Tsarevich and Tsarevna returned. Then a footman approached Lydia with a message that Captain Chirnov was waiting downstairs.

Here they met Sergei, already cloaked, and flanked by two servants holding the ladies' wraps. Outside, Kira got into the sleigh waiting for her. A rug was tucked around her and she was taken back to Sergei's house for the inevitable scolding before being sent home. She was feeling somewhat deflated. Lydia's abuse left her unmoved but she was distressed at hurting her brother who so clearly hated Prince Alexis. Contrary to her belief the two did know each other years ago when Alexis was also in the same famous regiment, and they must have quarrelled bitterly.

I ought to have asked the Prince if

he knew Sergei. Why didn't she? As the name was familiar to Alexis, why did he not claim previous acquaintance? He had not done so either to herself or to her father.

When they reached the house, Lydia declared herself to be so upset by the evening's disturbance that she had a violent headache and must go to bed immediately.

"You talk to your sister," she said ungraciously to Sergei, who professed great concern about his wife.

The scene appeared somewhat artificial to Kira. She sensed that Lydia merely wanted to shift the onus of scolding on Sergei, and she was rather glad. It seemed so long since she had been given an opportunity to talk unreservedly with this beloved brother. With no Lydia at hand, he would see reason.

She made a polite beginning.

"I am sorry Lydia has a bad headache."

"Apart from your foolish behaviour, Kira, she is overcome by the memory of her dead brother, Prince Ivan Granovski. Like me we were in the Preobrajenski with Prince Alexis Dolgoruky. In fact the two fought a duel."

"I thought Prince Ivan died from smallpox."

"Yes, he did — some time afterwards. Oh, there were no fatal consequences regarding the duel, which was unfinished though Prince Ivan would have won. Our colonel intervened, and Prince Alexis being what we all know him to be — only I can hardly explain to an innocent girl like you . . . "

"Never mind my innocence, Sergei. I have the right to know why you and Lydia are so set against Prince Alexis. Is it because he is the brother of the Tsar's mistress and the only member of that family who remains friendly with her? I have been to the Winter Palace with him. The Princess Catherine Dolgoruky wished to thank me for saving her life. Oh, you did not know until tonight that I did that. I was walking in the Summer Garden and saw a Nihilist raising a revolver, but I caught his arm and the bullet missed its aim."

Sergei looked too dumbfounded to speak. Kira added, "Papa gave me permission to go to the Winter Palace. In fact he encouraged Prince Alexis to visit our house regularly, and talk about astronomy."

"Astronomy indeed!"

There was a world of scorn in Sergei's voice.

"He invited us to the Pulkova Observatory, and we went."

"The cunning devil! All this was done with the intention of aggravating me, I'll be bound!"

"Why, Sergei? Is it anything to do with what happened between the two of you years ago? If so, you must tell me. And doesn't Papa know?"

"My God! He must not."

"What happened?" persisted Kira. Her brother was still hesitating. She went on asking questions. "I suppose your quarrel, or whatever it was, took place while Papa was away in Russian America as he is ignorant of it? Did you get into a bad scrape?"

"Not a scrape," Sergei hastened to assure her, though he looked embarrassed. "You know how fussy Papa is about gambling."

"I have never heard him speak on the subject."

"Being a girl you wouldn't."

"You don't gamble, do you?"

"My dear girl, all officers in the Preobrajenski and other regiments do. Oh, I keep within sensible limits now." This was a lie, but Kira did not realise it. He went on, "While Papa was in Russian America, I did get involved. I had to live up to Granovski standards because I wanted to become formally betrothed to Lydia on Papa's return when his consent could be obtained. Now, of course, I keep within limits I can afford, as I have just told you."

"But what has this to do with what you did years ago?"

"I have no wish for Papa to know how foolish I was years ago. Now, Kira, can I rely on you to keep your mouth shut about the past?"

"Of course, but I still don't understand how Prince Alexis is concerned."

"Lydia's brother challenged him to a duel and I had to support Prince Ivan by acting as second. We had a colonel who was anxious to stamp out duelling and had threatened to expel any officers who took part in one. Because of that dastardly Prince Alexis, I nearly got booted out of the Preobrajenski."

"Why you?"

"As a second, of course. I acted in that capacity for Prince Ivan."

"What about Prince Alexis and Lydia's brother who were actually going to fight?"

"They did fight, but neither had wounded the other when the duel was stopped. The four of us were hauled up for reproof."

"Who was the fourth."

"A fool who stood second for that rogue Prince Alexis."

Kira struggled to get the position clear but she was still confused by her brother's explanations, which she found very muddled.

"You said your colonel had threatened to expel any officers who fought in duels. Did he let you all off then?"

Sergei had escaped such a disgrace, and she had never heard of it happening to Lydia's dead brother. In fact Lydia always spoke as if smallpox had carried off a man who would have been a great military commander had he lived long enough for his genius to mature.

"We were pardoned for the duel, but Alexis Dolgoruky was turned out because he had proved himself to be a card-cheat. It was because of that the duel was begun. Such a dastardly action was unworthy of any officer in the Preobrajenski."

"A card-cheat! How?"

"He was playing against Prince Ivan, but Ivan became suspicious that certain cards were marked, challenged him, and — well, I was watching the game and examined them. Another officer joined us and he found the faint marks too."

"Was Prince Alexis losing then?"

"No, winning — winning vast sums, and unfairly. Surely you realise, Kira, that any man who behaves in that dastardly fashion is an out-and-out rotter. The colonel would have made a public example of him, but being a ward of the Tsar the affair was hushed up."

"Prince Alexis somewhat resembles the Tsar."

"You've noticed that, or have you heard gossip?"

"I've heard nothing, but there is a likeness. Do you mean that . . . "

"Hush! It is not wise to voice such suspicions where His Imperial Majesty is concerned, but Alexis is believed to be the product of an affair between the Tsar and a Hessian governess the Tsarina brought from her own country. The woman died in childbirth. The late Prince Michael Dolgoruky was an intimate friend of His Majesty, so what could be more convenient than to get the baby adopted into that family? Still, a girl like you, Kira, should not know about such matters."

"I am eighteen," said Kira stoutly. "But this adoption must have happened before the Tsar took his present mistress."

Sergei gave a sardonic laugh.

"Considering the Winter Palace slut is only two years older than her card-cheating brother, it certainly did. The Tsar started to have affairs on the side a few years after his much vaunted love marriage to the present Tsarina, but he behaved with decorum until he installed Catherine Dolgoruky under the same roof as his wife, a thing no man should do. Fancy Papa letting you visit!"

"The Princess sent for me."

"She is not Tsarina yet."

"Do you think she will be, Sergei?"

"The present Tsarina Marie is very sickly. When she dies, anything may happen."

Kira repeated what her father had said about it being wrong to criticise the Tsar's actions since God had created him monarch of Russia. Sergei gave a contemptuous snort. She changed the subject by asking if Prince Alexis were forced to leave the regiment after his card-cheating was exposed with discovery of the unfinished duel.

"He was, but allowed to do so quietly because of the Tsar's personal intervention. Without acknowledging Alexis as his son, His Majesty has always taken a special interest in him. Certainly he consented to that coward's wish to quit military life and study at a university abroad. Alexis went to England, I know, took up this ridiculous astronomy, and now lives at Pulkova. Did you say he had the nerve to take you and Papa to see the Observatory?"

"Papa was interested, and so was I. Oh, Sergei, I really cannot believe Prince Alexis acted so meanly as to cheat Lydia's brother at cards. Are you sure there was no mistake?"

"There was no mistake," replied Sergei in a thunderous voice that quite alarmed Kira.

He began to pace up and down the room.

"Alexis Dolgoruky had been suspected previously of that practice. On this occasion I saw him mark three cards with a pin he took from his cravat. All thought out beforehand, you see! However little you know about the world, Kira, even you can realise such a man is unworthy of your acquaintance. That Summer Garden incident — and Lydia and I had no idea you were involved in it — well, as I say, I wish to God you had not been walking in the place just then."

"The Princess Dolgoruky would have been killed."

Sergei made no comment on that, but Kira saw him compress his lips. He then went back to his original theme, namely that her behaviour at the Anitchkov Palace tonight had been lamentable, ending with insisting she had nothing more to do with Prince Alexis. The acquaintance formed, and permitted through her father's ignorance of the prince's true character, must be dropped straightaway.

"Papa will wonder why I have suddenly become unfriendly. I shall be obliged to explain about the card-cheating."

"Oh, you are not to do that."

"I don't see how I can avoid it."

"Not for my sake?"

He touched Kira on her most vulnerable spot for she dearly loved Sergei. It grieved her he had not married a woman whom she could love too, but try as hard as she could she could not care for Lydia. Nor did her father, for that matter, but it vexed the Count that after ten years of marriage there had been no children. Lydia née Granovski had produced no heir to the Chirnov title and estates.

Sergei now took the view that Prince Alexis would not dare to approach the Count or Kira again.

"He is too much in dread of me to

aggravate, my displeasure. Oh, he will scuttle back to Pulkova to his stars and telescope!"

"He does some work as well at Petersburg Observatory. That is how he was in the Summer Garden with Princess Dolgoruky and her children. He makes a great fuss of the children."

"Being officially their uncle! Then he must please the Tsar by being the only person to remain friendly with his so-called sister. Oh, there may be a few other toad-eaters, but I have heard no less a personage than the Tsarevna say, the Princess must be the loneliest woman in Petersburg."

"Poor creature!"

"Her troubles are of her own making," was Sergei's unsympathetic comment, and he sounded just like Lydia when he made it.

"Does Prince Alexis often come to Court?" asked Kira.

"Heavens no! I should imagine the Tsar does not wish comments on the physical resemblance between them. Oh, this evening was an unprecedented exception, by His Majesty's whim to annoy the

Tsarevich and Tsarevna in every possible way. Look how he consistently spoke German, and the Tsarevich, loyal to the Panslavism movement, was fuming with anger."

"So inconsistent when the Tsarina was a princess of Hesse."

"But the Tsarevich resents his father's nonsense about opening up links with the West. Now, Kira, you be very distant with that scoundrel if by any chance he does call upon Papa. By the way, Lydia heard from the Tsarevna that when Tsarina Marie returns, as she will this month, you will be an extra Maid of Honour. The Tsar has ordered your name to be added to the imperial household list."

"Yes, Papa told me the same just before I set off for the reception. I suppose I may have to take up residence at the Winter Palace before he leaves for Bulgaria."

"Assuredly you will. And serving the Tsarina means you will have no contact with the mistress on the third floor, or her so-called brother."

Kira could well believe that. Marie of Hesse loved her husband so deeply that she would submit to an order like taking Kira as Maid of Honour, but she never saw Princess Dolgoruky, nor did her husband expect that. As for Prince Alexis, he would also be excluded from her presence. She would not want to receive a man conceived by her husband and another woman, nor one friendly with the reigning mistress.

Sergei continued to blacken Prince Alexis's character while Kira listened meekly, hoping to conceal her painful feeling of complete disillusionment. In spite of her limited knowledge of male leisure pursuits, she was aware card-cheating was a despicable practice. She could never forgive, far less love, someone guilty of such conduct, and she regretted the encouragement she had innocently given towards friendship. If anyone but Sergei had told her she was sure she could not have believed it.

Kira never doubted Sergei's word, or his judgment — at least judgment uninfluenced by Lydia. At the card-playing, Lydia was not of course present. She only heard about it afterwards.

"Give me your solemn promise not to

109

betray me to Papa. I mean I do not want him to know I was nearly thrown out of the regiment for acting as second in a duel when duels were forbidden."

"But you were not expelled. And the affair happened years ago. Why, you could have barely been twenty."

"Please, Little Sister!"

When he called her that, how could she do otherwise than make the promise? Oh, he was a dear, dear brother! He kissed her most affectionately as he parted with her. Lydia had not really detached him from his family, she thought, as the sleigh took her home.

There her personal maid Anna was waiting to undress her, and Kira was so weary she expected to fall asleep immediately her head touched the pillow. However, she lay awake, tossing and turning until dawn, then fell into a deep sleep, only roused by Anna bringing her chocolate far later than the usual hour.

"You looked so worn out I let you sleep on," explained the maid. "And not much better are you now, Kira Vassilievna. Didn't you enjoy the grand reception at the Anitchkov Palace?"

"No, I did not, but I don't want to answer any questions."

So the toilette was completed in silence and the maid dismissed. Kira went to a window and surveyed the wintry scene. The sun was shining, not brilliantly but quite strongly for early January, and she considered whether or not she should ring and order Mischa to bring a sleigh to the front door. The old coachman would drive, of course, and she should sit back letting the cold frosty air sting her cheeks while her body was kept cosily warm under thick fur rugs. The sleigh would glide along on its runners, its silver bells tinkling, and the sound might soothe that inner hurt which was as painful as it was last night.

She rang for Anna to pass on the order, then to help her put on outdoor garments. Anna was a few minutes answering the bell. When she entered her plain peasant face was alight with excitement.

"The Prince Alexis Dolgoruky has called. He and the master are talking together in the drawing-room."

If only she had made up her mind sooner and gone out before he arrived!

Now she felt trapped. Could she slip off without being noticed, or was it safer to remain in her bedchamber?

Then the door opened and she heard her father enquiring if she were there. Might he come in? A voice, unlike her own, said quaveringly, "Yes, Papa." Anna placed a chair for Count Chirnov, then vanished.

"I have a morning caller. He is waiting to see you in the drawing-room alone, Kira. As is proper, he came to ask my permission first, and although somewhat premature, I think you can guess his business. Prince Alexis Dolgoruky is requesting to be considered as a suitor for your hand in marriage."

5

THERE was complete silence in the room. Kira tried to say no, and her lips formed the words but she could not utter them, while she sat rigid, conscious her father was regarding her with a smile of approval mingled with pride.

"You must have perceived Prince Alexis's admiration, my dear. I gather this was very marked at the Anitchkov Palace, and that you were encouraging. Encouraging with propriety, of course. He himself realises his offer is a little precipitate, but he is obliged to return to Pulkova this week and he knows I shall be leaving for Bulgaria immediately after the Celebrations, so he felt it only right to speak to me. I assured him of my approval. He has all the qualities I could desire in a husband for you."

Kira was dumbfounded. The irony of such a proposal, which once she might have welcomed, but was abhorrent after

113

Sergei's revelations!

"Prince Alexis is waiting in the drawing-room. You may see him alone and tell him how welcome is his proposal."

"But it is not," burst out Kira.

The silence that followed was for a single minute, but it seemed a far longer period of time to Kira. The air was pregnant with tension. Then Count Chirnov spoke.

"I cannot have heard you aright, or is this your notion of feminine coyness? You cannot seriously mean that Prince Alexis's proposal of marriage is unwelcome to you."

"Yes, Papa, that is what I do mean."

"Impossible!"

"Impossible for me, Papa, to accept the Prince as a husband."

"You are refusing to accept Prince Alexis," exclaimed Count Chirnov in a tone of incredulity. "What mad notion is this?"

If only she could tell her father of her utter disillusionment but to do that would have meant breaking her promise to Sergei.

She said feebly, "I cannot like him

well enough to give myself to him in marriage."

"You appeared to like him, in fact show him particular favour when he was a frequent caller after that Summer Garden incident, and when he entertained us at Pulkova Observatory. I believed then that you were partial to him. As for last night at the Anitchkov Palace, he seems to have been given a wrong impression of your sentiments if they were what you now say they are."

"I am very sorry," murmured Kira guiltily.

She had cast down her eyes, afraid to look at her father. In a kinder, but perplexed, tone of voice he said her attitude was beyond comprehension.

"I am inclined to think you do not know your own feelings, Kira."

But she herself was sure she did. Twenty-four hours ago she might have hesitated and pleaded for time. If this offer had come the same evening, after their waltz together, Kira would have had no doubt in her heart. When Sergei and Lydia appeared she was on the verge of falling in love with Alexis.

Then came the revelation of his past which killed all former regard. A mean card-cheat! A man despised by Sergei, the brother whose opinion could not be at fault. How she longed to tell Papa the truth. Then he would stop treating her like a silly coy maiden. Fancy telling her she did not know the strength of her sentiments! Yes, she had sentiments which were the reverse of what he believed they were.

"I was not happy for you to come out under Lydia's tutelage," the Count was saying. "Although born into the noble family of Granovski, she has never been a favourite of mine, and I wished I had not been obliged to entrust your coming-out in society to her. Your dear mother would have managed matters so differently. I feared Lydia might push you into the arms of any gentleman she found suitable, and knowing her lack of discernment I was prepared to refuse my consent to any unworthy choice. Therefore I was delighted when Prince Alexis made our acquaintance and, from the start, so clearly admired you. I wish my own son were more like him."

116

"You cannot be referring to Sergei, Papa!"

"Sergei has not turned out as I wished. It was unfortunate your mother and I were obliged to be in Russian America during the most critical period of his youth."

"But Papa, he is highly esteemed in his regiment. He has already attained the rank of captain . . . "

"I know, I know! Never mind Sergei. Cannot you appreciate what a brilliant and unusual man is the Prince? He is an astronomer, a man of learning. I thought you took an interest in his work, certainly as intelligent an interest as could be shown by a young lady with no previous knowledge of the subject."

"I found it fascinating, Papa, to visit the Pulkova Observatory and to look through a telescope, but I wasn't thinking of attracting the Prince."

"You gave every evidence of enjoying his companionship. That is a basis for marriage. Your mother and I were intimate friends as well as being joined in matrimony by the Holy Church."

"I could never feel for Prince Alexis as

I am sure Mama did for you."

"Nonsense!"

"I know I cannot marry Prince Alexis Dolgoruky, Papa."

The anger in her father's eyes made Kira's heart sink. She was displeasing him by her refusal. This was going to erect a barrier between them, for he was determined to see no flaw in Alexis. Like herself until Sergei made his revelations, Papa had fallen a victim to plausible manner and charm.

"I am extremely disappointed in you, Kira."

Since the day she saved Princess Catherine Dolgoruky's life, Papa and she had grown closer, just as when she was a small child before the Smolny Nobility School had cut her off from him and, to a certain extent, from her mother. Now there was going to be another barrier between them, and could that be wondered at since her father did not know the true character of the man seeking her hand? Was there no hint she could give to enlighten him?

Her father's voice broke into her thoughts.

"Prince Alexis is waiting downstairs to see you." Sensing unwillingness on his daughter's part, he added, "It is your duty to give him your decision."

Kira guessed the Count was thinking she might alter that decision when confronted with the would-be suitor. They walked along the landing and down the staircase, but in the hall Count Chirnov merely indicated the closed door of the drawing-room. He waved away a footman about to open it.

"This is an occasion for two people to discuss their mutual sentiments alone." And as if endeavouring to mask his belief in Kira changing her mind, he added, "I will see the Prince in my bookroom afterwards, and I hope you with him."

Kira watched him walk away in the direction of his private study that he called the bookroom. It was a nuisance that Sergei was so determined the card-cheating and duel must be kept from Papa. If he knew the truth, then he would no longer blame her refusal.

She entered the drawing-room, expecting to find Alexis elated with success at having obtained permission to address her, and confident of her eager acceptance. She must have shown marked encouragement to prompt this premature offer. Of course it was not a proposal of marriage, but the obvious prelude to such, and what gossips called 'A settled thing.'

Hands clasped tightly behind her back made it clear she had no intention of permitting the gentleman to take one of her hands, kiss it and bow. That was the usual conventional greeting, but not in this case! She glared at him with hostile eyes and lips set in anger, and his response to this was different from what she had anticipated.

Instead of showing surprise, he said calmly, "I thought Sergei Vassilievich might try to poison your mind against me after I had left the Anitchkov Palace. Now listen to my defence."

"I will not. Your defence does not interest me. I am here by my father's orders to give an answer to your request to pay me the — er — addresses preliminary to matrimony. Well, my answer is no."

"I admit I have spoken to your father somewhat prematurely, but I understand you will shortly be entering the Tsarina's household. Hearing that and knowing you would be inaccessible unless I had your father's permission to see you as my betrothed, I realised I must not delay informing him of my love for you."

"Love! You don't love me!"

"But I do. I think I have since that awful scene in the Summer Garden when we first met."

"That is unfortunate because I cannot possibly return your love, not after what my brother has told me about your past."

"Let me explain . . . "

"No, I will not listen."

"Kira Vassilievna, surely you will give me a fair hearing so that I can refute Sergei's lies. Yes, he must have lied to you."

"A fair hearing! Sergei lie! He would never do that. He said you were forced to leave the Preobrajenski because you cheated at cards. My sister-in-law's brother, Prince Ivan Granovski, found you out. Sergei was present and he examined the cards you had marked."

"Oh, Sergei examined those cards,"

declared Alexis, and his lips curled in contempt.

"You acknowledge your crime then. I only wish I could tell the truth to Papa, but Sergei thinks — well, Papa knows nothing and disclosure would distress him, Sergei says."

"How considerate of Sergei Vassilievich," and again Alexis's tone was contemptuous.

Kira pressed on.

"Papa insisted on my seeing you alone. He cannot understand my refusal to receive your advantageous offer. Oh, I know he has granted you the permission you sought, but it is in my power to refuse to listen to your protestations of love. I want nothing further to do with you, Highness. Go back to your astronomy."

"Does that mean you accept your brother's account of an incident that took place years ago, and without hearing what I have to say in defence?"

"There can be no defence. You cheated at cards and were caught. That is enough for me."

"I came prepared to find Sergei had forestalled me, but I believed you would do me the justice of asking me for my explanation. Please do."

"No, I will not."

"This is inconceivable."

Kira was unmoved. "I believe the brother whom I have known and respected all my life."

"Your lives have gone along different paths. There is a big difference in age, too. He was a soldier when you were a schoolgirl. As it is, you have very little worldly experience."

Kira thought he meant in a geographical sense, and reminded Alexis she had been to Russian America, Siberia, and Salonika.

"Periods when you were quite cut off from Sergei, therefore you cannot lay claim to know him well. I was with him for a considerable time at a military academy and in a military regiment."

"You cannot know him as well as I do," said Kira.

She turned to another aspect of the situation.

"Yesterday evening you put me in a conspicuous position by dancing three times in succession. Sergei said it was done to anger him. For the same reason you decided to see my father today. Your presumption is abominable. It would serve you right if Sergei told our father the truth."

"Truth? What truth?"

"If he branded you as the card-cheater you really are."

"Indeed, but I don't see Sergei doing that."

"He is too noble."

At this remark, Alexis burst out laughing. Kira was furious. She moved forward to ring a bell for a servant when her hand was gripped. For a moment Alexis's anger terrified her.

"Almighty God! I was confident, Kira, that you would ask to hear my version of that card affair before you blindly accepted Sergei's account."

"But Sergei's account can be the only true one. He does not lie, and I have no wish to listen to excuses you may invent. Sergei said you were plausible. Now I see how right he was."

"Little fool!"

"How dare you speak to me like that. I demand an instant apology."

Alexis said quietly, "Yes, I was rude and for my rudeness I apologise."

"I accept your apology, but I want nothing more to do with you. My father is waiting in the bookroom and he is desirous of seeing you before you leave this house."

"A house I shall never enter again," said Alexis.

Then he suddenly seized her, bent her head backwards as he kissed her quite brutally. It was a fierce, vicious kiss. Then she was alone.

Never had Kira felt so miserable. She began to think she had really been in love with Alexis during that waltz, and though the unmasking of his character by Sergei had been necessary, yet it was hard to bear the end of an illusion. But bear it she must. Prince Alexis Dolgoruky had gone out of her life for ever. Tears welled up in her eyes. This would not do. If she must cry, at least she would do it in the safety of her bedchamber.

Meanwhile Alexis was talking to Count Chirnov in the bookroom. The Count did not conceal his disappointment over Kira's obstinacy in refusing such a desirable offer from such a fine man.

"I fail to understand her, but then I never have. You know what it is in a family, Prince. The sons are close to the father and the daughters to the mother."

Alexis politely murmured agreement. None of his supposed brothers and sisters were close to the reckless Prince Michael Dolgoruky whose mind was occupied with fantastic building schemes on his estate. They alone gave him satisfaction and they swallowed up his fortune. His wife died before him, so it was fortunate the Tsar appointed himself guardian of all the children, including Alexis; who was never publicly acknowledged as 'half-imperial' but learnt this when he was a small boy, by what means he never quite knew. But servants talked when the vast country estate of Tioplovka was sold to pay the late Prince Michael's debts, the Tsar sending the Dolgoruky boys to military establishments and the girls to the Smolny Nobility School.

Alexander II only started to pay special attention to Alexis when the latter became involved in the interrupted duel with

Prince Ivan Granovski, with its probable expulsion from the Preobrajenski regiment. For the first time, father and son had a private interview when, reluctantly, Alexis was obliged to confess what had really happened. He was sorry for the foolish, extravagant Sergei Chirnov, whose alliance with the grand Granovski family was in jeopardy. Alexis hated military life, preferring one of study. He had not expected understanding from the autocratic Tsar, who scolded his son for behaving like 'one of those foolish mediaeval knight errants,' but the scold lacked force since Alexander II was by nature a man of peace, a reformer, and had been compelled to follow army training against his inclination. However, he had no choice but to fit into the mould destined for Heir Apparent and future ruler of Russia.

Alexis is like Nicholas, the Tsar muttered to himself, and here he was thinking of his eldest son, Tsarevich Nicholas, who had died of consumption four years earlier. This bastard standing before him was another Nicholas, whereas the five living sons born in wedlock,

127

especially the present Tsarevich Alexander, longed to become commanders in wars the Tsar secretly hoped to avoid. Russia must be great, but through negotiation and diplomacy, not through bloody battles. Alexander II had an inward loathing of what he considered barbaric occupation of uncivilised nations, but all his life he had been obliged to conceal this from father, tutors, and others about him. His heart warmed to the young man who wanted to leave the Preobrajenski and lead a civilised life.

"How do you propose to occupy your time?"

"It has always been my wish to study science and mathematics at a university."

"Why did you not tell me that before?"

"I thought you wanted me to be a military man and I did not want to disappoint you. Now I have lost the chance of that career by becoming involved with Chirnov, I beg you to let me follow my inclination."

"As you wish. You shall be free from a military career, and instead study subjects of your own choice at a university. I respect your confidence and will keep it, although I disapprove of you sacrificing your good name in the regiment for that contemptible Sergei Vassilievich Chirnov. He deserves no consideration."

"His father has been in Russian America for a number of years, Sire, and Sergei is anxiously awaiting the return for consent to his betrothal to Princess Lydia Granovski. She would not forgive him for fighting her brother, so if I forced Sergei to own he marked the cards, then the match would be off. I had to take the blame and fight Prince Ivan myself."

The truth was that Sergei, desperately in debt, marked certain cards in order to win from Prince Ivan Granovski. He rose from the table having gained heavily, and with his subterfuge undiscovered. Alexis took his place, won a single game but without realising what Sergei had done. He gained no advantage from the pin scratchings, which were very faint, because he did not know they were there. His victory was perfectly fair, only a fellow officer came to watch, noticed a mark on an ace of clubs, and called Prince Ivan's attention to it.

Then followed discovery, challenge to a duel, and later Sergei's private pleading with Alexis not to betray him 'or I shall lose a wealthy bride.' Good-naturedly and somewhat rashly, Alexis allowed himself to be considered the culprit.

The Tsar did not like Alexis bearing the blame for a fault he had not committed, but he admired the gallantry which prompted that action.

"I wish the object of your sacrifice were more worthy," he remarked.

"Sergei is now clear of debt, Sire, and he has solemnly promised me to restrict gambling to what he can afford."

"Does that mean you gave him additional money?"

"No, Sire, I only agreed to take the blame and fight the duel on condition he made that promise. He is terrified of losing the Princess Lydia, or disillusioning his father, who will soon be back from the east."

"I hold Count Chirnov in very high esteem, which was why I chose him for the mission to Russian America." In speaking informally to his son the Tsar had dropped the imperial 'we'. He continued, "The Count is a valued old friend so I do not wish to see his son disgraced. I do not like this expulsion from the regiment for you, but if you are averse to a life of soldiering I cannot refuse your request. I shall see the affair is hushed up."

Alexis attended Cambridge University, studied and practised astronomy at Greenwich, and was now at Pulkova, where he spent most of his time. Intimacy developed between him and the man who was really his father; and when Princess Catherine Dolgoruky became the Tsar's mistress, her supposed brother visited her and was like a real uncle to her children. Now, by an extraordinary quirk of fate, Alexis had come into contact with the young sister of his former treacherous friend, and had fallen ardently in love with her. But, as he walked towards Count Chirnov's bookroom and thought of Kira's lack of faith in him, and blind faith in her brother's merits, he felt that love had received a mortal blow.

She never gave me a chance to defend myself. That was his complaint. Then he was ashamed of his display of passion in seizing and kissing her violently against her will.

Oh, well, that was the end! She would never forget the poison Sergei had pumped into her mind, and thinking what an easy prey she had been, even in the case of a beloved brother, Alexis was angry over her acceptance of his being in the wrong. Oh, he was better off without such a weak woman!

Count Chirnov was disappointed by the suitor's lack of success.

"Try again in a week or so. I'll talk to her . . . "

"I entreat Your Excellency not to influence Kira in any way. Let us leave the matter in abeyance. For the present I am certain it is wiser to let her consider the matter as she feels able." Not that Alexis believed she would, but he could not tell Count Chirnov what had ruined the love-affair — namely, the contemptible falseness of Sergei. "I shall return to Pulkova."

"But you will be back soon. Don't be daunted, Prince. Kira will soon come to her senses. I mean, she is a sensible girl, and an obedient one."

"This is hardly a matter of obedience, Your Excellency. Surely you would not wish her to marry a man she did not love."

"Of course not, and I have told her I should never be that type of father. But she loves you. I am convinced of it."

"Give her time, I entreat Your Excellency."

The last remark mollified the old man. He interpreted it as indicating that Prince Alexis intended to persevere, but then Count Chirnov had no idea of the real issues involved.

6

ALEXIS alighted from his troika at a side door of the Winter Palace, was saluted by the guard on duty, and went inside. He passed other guards stationed in the lofty halls, and was at last able to escape from them — those halls made him feel he was in a cathedral — and turn into a private part where he ascended two quite imposing staircases, although neither was a principal one. His own rooms were on the third floor, though some distance from the closed apartments set aside for Princess Catherine Dolgoruky and her children. He only used them when duty brought him to Petersburg.

On the table of his sitting-room was a note.

"From the Princess Dolgoruky," explained the manservant who waited on him. "It is urgent."

However the message was only a request for him to call and see her as soon as he could, for the 'little ones' were longing to play with him before their bedtime.

Alexis had not realised it was so late in the afternoon. In January darkness came early, and, although conscious that the sun had set, he had hardly been aware he had been driving round and round Petersburg in a fury after leaving the Chirnov house.

The guard on duty admitted him to the Princess's suite, and after greeting his supposed sister, he spent nearly an hour romping with Gogo, pet name for the young George, and Olga. The second girl, Catherine, was a few years younger than Olga and still languid from a bout of pneumonia. The Tsar had suggested the child be sent away from this city of fogs, but her mother was too afraid of separation. Since the incident in the Summer Garden, she was in perpetual fear lest an assassin deprive her of lover or children.

Brother and sister in name only, yet in upbringing, Alexis took the same vow as Count Chirnov that the Tsar was above criticism and it angered him that other members of the Dolgoruky family should treat Catherine as an outcast. They never sought admission to the Winter Palace suite, nor did they communicate with her by letter. She declared herself indifferent to this boycott, telling Alexis she counted the world well lost for love, but he sensed she had periods of depression brought on by isolation.

Work kept him at Pulkova, with occasional visits to Petersburg, and when he came to the capital he made a point of calling on her, while he made a great fuss of the three children she had borne the Tsar. In fact it was easier to play with them than hold a conversation with their mother, who had very little to say for herself. As Kira had noticed, the princess was quite knowledgeable about astronomy, but Kira did not realise an effort had been made because of the Tsar's interest in his son's work. The Tsar paid several private visits to Pulkova Observatory, and took Princess Dolgoruky with him, also the elder children.

This afternoon Alexis found Gogo and Olga with their mother and thankfully joined in pretending to be a bear. The game helped to banish from his thoughts the painful rejection of his suit by Kira. It had been no consolation to brand her as unjust and — yes, weak, to listen to Sergei's untrue version without giving him a hearing.

At last the children were led away by nurses for the supper that preceded their bedtime, and Alexis was left alone with Catherine. He was surprised to hear her ask how he enjoyed last night's reception at the Anitchkov Palace, because her exclusion from society meant that she never attended any function, large or small, so had no desire to hear about any. This was certainly an exception.

"His Imperial Majesty gave me a full account last night after he returned here."

Catherine always gave her lover this title when speaking of him, even to Alexis. Sometimes she actually addressed the Tsar as Majesty, though as a general rule she used the pet name of Sasha, an abbreviation of Alexander.

"His Imperial Majesty declared he had been quite naughty in teasing the pan-Russian Tsarevich, who commands that

Russian, only, be spoken in his house, but nobody can command the Tsar of Russia. So he spoke German, and the Tsarevich looked furious but dared not complain."

"Oh, the Tsarevich is impossibly narrow, especially as his own mother is German. How can a princess of Hesse be anything else?"

Catherine raised one shoulder pettishly at mention of the Tsarina, for while Alexander II's consort was alive there was no possibility of a morganatic marriage between her and her beloved.

She said spitefully, "The married woman is coming here next week, dragging herself away from the Riviera sunshine."

"She is a sick woman."

Alexis's remark was ignored. Catherine went on, "I suppose she will be escorted from the Riviera by the Grand Dukes Sergei and Paul. How she keeps those two younger sons from fulfilling their military duties just because she likes to have them idling around her! Such a bad example!"

"I wonder the Tsar allows it, but

his word is absolute, even in the Preobrajenski."

"You would not have been expelled if you had let him interfere, but you said you preferred university study to military life."

"Which was true, and I wished I had been brave enough to say that years before. I could have escaped from what I hated, but I never thought of confessing my point of view to His Majesty. I did not know him as well as I do now."

Catherine gave a little laugh.

"So you waited for that Chirnov rat to transfer the burden of his misdeeds on you. Yes, His Imperial Majesty was telling me the story last night. I had no idea when I summoned Kira Chirnov to thank her for saving the lives of myself and my children."

"And what exactly did His Majesty say last night?"

"Well, he told me how that dreadful Captain Chirnov took advantage of your generosity, and he would not have permitted it only you vowed you would be thankful to leave the Preobrajenski. He said how he hated military training, but as Heir Apparent he had no choice."

"Really! And what else?"

"I don't think His Imperial Majesty would mind my repeating to you, Alexis, how bitterly he resented fate which forced him to take the formal Oath of Allegiance on his sixteenth birthday. Then he realised what lay ahead, that he might have to plunge Russia into war when all he wanted for her was peace and reform."

"He has been a great reformer. He abolished serfdom."

"He wanted to do more, and still hopes to, but there have been wars he deplored . . . Oh, he would have preferred a life spent in study, such as he has secured for you."

There was a short silence. Then Catherine said in a lighter tone, "So His Imperial Majesty arranged for you to dance the polonaise with Kira Chirnov. I hear you were most attentive after that, and would have continued, only His Imperial Majesty could endure the Tsarevich and the Tsarevna no longer, and he left, followed naturally by his two aides-de-camp. Are you seriously interested in the girl, Alexis?"

"I was, but now I am not."

"What on earth do you mean?"

"She accepts implicitly her brother's lying version of why I left the Preobrajenski."

"Hasn't she been told the truth?"

"She would not believe me. I could see it was waste of time to try. Besides, Catherine, I have no desire to marry a woman who can so easily be swayed by a brother. I return to Pulkova tomorrow, if the Tsar permits, and already the Kira Vassilievna Chirnov has passed out of my life."

The pain of damaged pride had been increasing since Alexis left Count Chirnov's bookroom, although he had given that nobleman the impression that he would continue to woo Kira and win her in time. He had not meant to give a mistaken impression, but he was concerned lest he revealed the cowardly behaviour of Sergei to a doting father, for Alexis concluded the Count was that. If he had known the Count was disappointed in his son, he might have been less inclined to keep the secret as Kira desired.

The affair was over, and he wished to escape from any future encounter with her.

Aloud he said, "As I just told you, I hope to return to Pulkova tomorrow."

"But His Imperial Majesty summoned you to Petersburg and he will not wish you to leave so soon."

"He wanted to hear about my astronomical work. It fascinates him. But the sooner I disappear the better, for the Tsarina will soon arrive. Other guests are expected at the Winter Palace for the Jubilee Celebrations; like Grand Duke Louis of Hesse and Prince Alexander of Bulgaria, and you know I shall be equally unacceptable to the brother and nephew of the Tsarina. Not that I have met either, but I am certain they know from Her Majesty about the Hessian governess who had a liaison with the Tsar, and of which I am the result."

It was tactless of Alexis to have said this, and the Princess Dolgoruky showed her annoyance by saying haughtily,

"Speaking of personal matters concerning His Imperial Majesty borders on treason."

Like your liaison, thought Alexis with grim humour. Aloud he said, "The Winter Palace is so enormous that it might be argued I could avoid royal personages to whom I am unwelcome, but the Tsar will be too occupied to talk about my astronomical researches. In the circumstances I cannot see him opposing my immediate return to Pulkova."

The Tsar entered just then, and Alexis rose, expecting dismissal in order that the lovers be alone, but after embracing Princess Dolgoruky, Alexander asked for his children. The little Catherine was already asleep, but he played with Gogo and Olga as gaily as his son had done earlier. When they had been taken back to the nursery, he turned his attention to Alexis.

"Have you called at Count Chirnov's today?"

"Yes, Sire."

The Tsar had told Alexis to address him thus in private, rather than use the title 'Majesty'. Sometimes Alexis knew instinctively 'Father' would have been preferred, but that revealed a relationship that might be known but must not be acknowledged.

"Did you see the young lady of whom you made such a conquest last night?"

"What happened at the Anitchkov Palace reception is relegated to the past for ever, Sire. I offered for Kira Vassilievna, obtained her father's approval, but when I saw her I found her brother had already given a completely untruthful account of the circumstances surrounding my duel with Granovski. She believed Sergei."

"That scoundrel! He should have been expelled from the Preobrajenski for card-cheating."

"It would have been difficult to prove his guilt and my innocence if I had denounced him. I played with the cards not knowing he had marked them."

"He would have confessed if challenged. Once the duel was reported to me I should have instituted a full enquiry, only you had begged me to let you shoulder the blame for the sake of his father, and I shrank from such news awaiting my dear old friend, Count Chirnov, when he arrived here from Russian America. I acted wrongly."

"But you forget how glad I was to relinquish the military life. I have been far happier in pursuing knowledge."

"Will you continue so? Perhaps you are not so attracted to the girl as I had assumed."

"The attraction she had for me has vanished, Sire. She would not listen to my defence. She believes her brother's lies implicitly."

"She has disillusioned you then?"

"Completely, and for always. Now have I your permission to leave for Pulkova in the morning?"

"Yes, of course," said the Tsar testily. He still could not leave the subject. "I would not have agreed to respect your wishes if I could have foreseen you would suffer years later. If only you had had a fellow officer to back you up at the time."

"I should have exacted secrecy from such a one, Sire."

"I believe you would!" was the exasperated exclamation, and this was followed by dismissal of Alexis with an order to present himself in the Tsar's study, which was in the official imperial apartments on a lower floor.

"I want a report on your latest discoveries concerning double stars."

A catalogue of those known to astronomers in 1820 had been published by the first Director of Pulkova before the Observatory was built; and since it started to function the work had continued, more and more such stars being found as the telescope there scanned the heavens.

Catherine had remarked on the Tsarina's return next week, and after Alexis had supplied a copy of the report, the Tsar put it aside for later perusal while he demanded abruptly if Alexis would be pleased to see Kira Vasselievna removed from the influence of Princess Lydia Chirnov and her husband, particularly while Count Chirnov was in Bulgaria.

"As I have stated, Sir, the young lady no longer means anything to me, but I certainly think a different environment from her brother's house would be advantageous."

The Tsar nodded.

"I spoke to the Count some time ago about Kira Vassilievna's name being added to Tsarina's Maids of Honour list. She will be taking up residence at the Winter Palace when Her Imperial Majesty arrives."

Alexis made no reply, only bowed deferentially and hoped to convey lack of interest by assuming a wooden expression. Since being ordered by the Tsar to accompany the monarch to the reception, then dance the polonaise with Kira, and encouraged to wait upon Count Chirnov that morning, he knew his imperial father was in favour of a match between him and Kira, therefore disappointed over its deathblow.

He experienced a certain satisfaction that she was not to be left with Sergei and his wife during the Count's absence in Bulgaria, although he doubted if attendance upon the invalid Tsarina would really remove her from their influence. They belonged to the Anitchkov Palace set and were favourites of the Tsarevich and Tsarevna, a couple beloved by the Tsarina. Surely the Tsar realised this. Of course His Imperial Majesty was anxious to do something for Kira when she had saved Princess Catherine Dolgoruky's life.

147

Kira Vassilievna is not my concern, Alexis told himself, believing it should soon banish her alluring image from his mind when he saw the shining silver domes of Pulkova and resumed the work he loved.

Before following Alexis to the study, the Tsar said to Catherine, "Kira Vassilievna shall be transferred to your household as soon as the Tsarina leaves Petersburg after the Celebrations. With you she will have opportunities of meeting Alexis. He will soon forgive her blind faith in that worthless brother. I wish I had exposed Sergei Vassilievich years ago, but I never dreamt that acceding to Alexis's request would bring trouble years later. It all seemed so unimportant at the time."

"Of course it did, Sasha darling."

Catherine always did agree with her lover, but she did not particularly want Kira transferred to her household when the Tsarina went abroad again. She would have to agree though. As it was, the prospect of the forthcoming Jubilee Celebrations was a source of irritation to her. She would be like a prisoner locked in a cell during the actual festivities; but this was the lot she had chosen, and during the period before she would not lack her lover's company in her secluded apartments. He was too bored with his sick wife to give Tsarina Marie much attention.

However, this consolation was denied Catherine, for arriving with the Tsarina was the Grand Duchess Marie, only daughter of the imperial couple, and doted upon by her father. While her brothers championed their mother in disapproval of Alexander II having his mistress in the Winter Palace, in spite of the Princess Dolgoruky's living in a separate set of apartments the Grand Duchess Marie maintained that the Tsar could do no wrong. She refused to join their condemnation.

"I love Papa, even more than my dear husband."

Her husband was Prince Alfred, Duke of Edinburgh, and second son of Queen Victoria. Marriage to him had meant living in England which, even after six years, she heartily loathed. Inordinately proud of being a grand duchess of Russia, she felt she was not given her due with regard to precedence and general importance there. It was delightful to come to Petersburg and be treated with proper reverence.

"The Grand Duchess Marie is expected at the same time as the Tsarina, and that quite soon," Count Chirnov informed his daughter.

She was doing her utmost to put Alexis out of her mind. It was not easy, especially as she had to endure Lydia's reproaches, including failure to give encouragement to Count Hippolyte Matvejevi.

"Do you realise he wishes to remarry as soon as it is proper? There must be a decent interval after his wife's death. He wants the second to be of good aristocratic birth. He has money in plenty, so though you will have an excellent dowry, that is not the first consideration. It would be with that so-called Dolgoruky."

Kira had found the best way to deal with her sister-in-law was to maintain a stony silence. Any attempt at argument provoked increased scolding. With Sergei it was different, but she found it difficult to get him alone. When she did he refused to disclose any further facts.

"I hear the adventurer has left Petersburg for Pulkova. His farce of star-gazing! Still I am thankful he is out of the way. I was afraid he might have the impudence to ask Papa for permission to address you, behaving as he did at the Anitchkov Palace. And with Papa having no idea what a scoundrel he is . . . "

"He did ask Papa. Papa was agreeable and told me he had given permission, but I was firm in refusing to receive any addresses from Prince Alexis Dolgoruky."

Then seeing her brother's face turn almost purple and hearing him gasp — he looked positively scared — Kira hastened to assure him she had betrayed nothing of any previous acquaintance, nor mentioned duel or card-cheating.

"I said I could not accept the Prince as a husband. Papa was angry, and still is."

This was only too true, but Kira did not say how distressing she found Count Chirnov's marked disapproval of her decision. She loved her father, maybe second to Sergei but very deeply, and she longed to be a comfort to him in his grief for the late Countess. She too missed her mother. And deep down was the lingering anguish for Alexis whom she could not respect after learning his true character.

"I trust you have not betrayed my confidence?"

Sergei still seemed alarmed and Kira hastened to reassure him.

"No, I have not said anything to Papa about your earlier relations with Prince Alexis Dolgoruky."

"Mind you don't."

"What must she not do?" asked Lydia, overhearing the last words as she entered the room.

"Blab to my father about that Dolgoruky villain."

"I should think not."

Lydia had just come from the Anitchkov Palace and was full of importance after hearing that the Tsarina Marie was expected in Petersburg the following Tuesday.

"Against medical advice, says the Tsarevna, who thinks her mother-in-law is very foolish. I understand, Kira, that you will be required to assume your new duties at the Winter Palace the day before, and I hope you have the sense to keep quiet about your unfortunate visit to the Tsar's mistress, and the woman's brother."

Count Chirnov's manner was stiff, in fact icy in its aloofness, when, later that day, he informed Kira about a message from the Winter Palace. As Lydia had said, the Tsarina was arriving on the next Tuesday, and the new Maid of Honour was to present herself the day before. When the time actually came, he did however escort her to the palace, but only as far as an entrance. Kira had a pass, but her father none, and there seemed no change in the strict security she had experienced when she was taken to see the Princess Dolgoruky.

"Good-bye, Papa, — well, for the present. I mean you will not be leaving for Bulgaria yet, will you?"

His face did soften as he replied, "Not until after the Jubilee Celebrations. I am to be presented to the Prince of Bulgaria when he attends them, and His Imperial Majesty wishes me to accompany the

Prince back to his country. But I shall see you before then, and certainly before I leave Russia."

"And you have no idea how long this mission in Bulgaria will take?"

"No, I have not, but I know now what the Tsar requires."

This was all the explanation Kira received. She entered the Winter Palace feeling very scared about her duties and the people she should meet, but found herself being well looked after and her bed-chamber comfortable although a little austere compared with the one at home. Not having seen the Tsarina for long, Kira was shocked at the ravages made by illness, and the extreme thinness of the hand extended for her to kiss.

"It must be four years since we last saw you at the Smolny."

Kira agreed, was then asked if she found life in Petersburg pleasant. She said yes, but that she had not experienced it for long owing to the period of mourning for her mother's death which occurred soon after leaving school. The Tsarina expressed sympathy over this bereavement, but the exertion of talking soon exhausted her and she was obliged to retire to her bedchamber to lie down. Taking charge was the Grand Duchess Marie, who not only ordered the new Maid of Honour to accompany her in attendance upon Her Majesty, but curtly dismissed the Tsarevna, who was also present.

"After that long tiring journey you need rest and quiet, Mama," declared the Grand Duchess.

Kira found her new life at the Winter Palace different from what she expected. Sickness made the ailing woman exacting and Kira as favourite Maid of Honour had practically no leisure time. She could not have gone to the third floor had she been inclined, while the great height of ceilings on lower floors effectively sealed off all sounds above. Definitely in command was the Grand Duchess Marie, who banned all visits except from the Tsar, and his were brief. Each day he appeared for about ten minutes in his wife's chamber. Kira was usually standing at the head of the bed, but Alexander took no more notice of her than if she had been a piece of furniture. Etiquette forbade her to speak unless addressed.

She kept her eyes mainly cast down, but managed to look at him surreptitiously now and then. Kira did not know enough about the Tsar as a person to realise he was a creature of moods, so could only marvel how different he was from the smiling monarch who used to visit the Smolny, and the teasing one at the Anitchkov Palace reception. She could see he hated the duty of making a visit to his wife, while to the Tsarina each one was the highlight of her day. Alexander shrank from those sensitive loving eyes which poured out affection he had once returned but now could not. The thraldom of Catherine Dolgoruky held him, and Marie knew it. There was no reproach in her eyes, only sad yearning.

"I am much better today."

That was her usual remark, also assurances she would not fail him when the Jubilee Celebrations began.

In the evenings, Kira was always the Maid of Honour chosen to sit with her, while the Grand Duchess dined alone with her father. On the third floor

Princess Dolgoruky suffered agonies of loneliness and envy.

The Tsarina was a considerate employer. She insisted on her four Maids of Honour being taken for a drive, and possibly a walk in the Summer Garden if the weather were suitable, but walks were few, for January and February were bitterly cold months. Kira was thankful for this. The Summer Garden was a place of such painful memories. Try as she would, it was impossible not to think about Prince Alexis, the man she could have loved had not Sergei revealed his real character.

Kept in close attendance on the Tsarina, Kira saw nothing of her brother and sister-in-law, nor of her father. Presumably Count Chirnov would leave for Bulgaria with Crown Prince Alexander, but she had no idea how long he would be absent; and before she left home for the Winter Palace his aloof manner made it clear he was still angry at her rejection of Prince Alexis. Kira had gathered that Bulgaria's new ruler required advice from a trusted servant of the Tsar, and remarks she heard from the Tsarina and the Grand Duchess merely confirmed this view.

Other European powers beside Russia wanted to interfere in Bulgarian affairs, and the Tsarina was interested because its ruler, chosen by the Tsar, was her nephew.

"I worry about Sandro. He is a fine soldier but quite inexperienced in the strategy of government."

"What does strategy matter in a barbaric place like that, Mama! The country has been part of the Turkish Empire for hundreds of years, so with christian government, such as Sandro will give it, there cannot be trouble."

"Supreme tact will be needed," sighed the Tsarina. She turned to Kira. "His Imperial Majesty was telling me that your father, Count Chirnov, has been appointed personal adviser to the Crown Prince."

The evening before the official start of the Jubilee Celebrations, when visiting royalties would have arrived, there was to be a grand banquet for such illustrious guests. The Tsar, who hitherto had ignored Kira because of vexation over her refusal of Prince Alexis, condescended to tell her that he had commanded her father to come to the Winter Palace that evening, wait until the banquet was over, 'so that we can present him to the Prince of Bulgaria.'

In his kindly fashion, he added, "While we are dining and the Tsarina has no need of your attendance, there will be an opportunity for you and your father to be alone."

But on the day of the banquet, it was obvious the sick Tsarina would be unable to be present, or to receive any guests. She had always been a martyr to migraine and this particularly severe attack kept her prostrate. Clinging to her favourite Kira's hand, she finally consented to take a morphine tablet prescribed by the physician, and administered by the Grand Duchess Marie. Dismissing all attendants except Kira, she waited until her mother fell into a drugged sleep.

"It was the strongest tablet Doctor Petritsky said he dare permit. Thank goodness it has worked."

The haughty Marie of Edinburgh actually spoke to Kira as if she were an equal. Dressed for the banquet in an evening gown of pale blue brocade and wearing a magnificent tiara of sapphires and diamonds, she looked every inch the daughter of Russia's ruler. The tiara had been a wedding present from the Tsar, and when she wore it in England Queen Victoria was always resentful of a daughter-in-law owning more jewels than herself.

"I must go to the salon and mingle with the guests," continued Marie. "The Grand Duke of Hesse and the Crown Prince of Bulgaria should have arrived by now and be with His Imperial Majesty. Apparently their train was late. Dinner, however, is to be served at six, so after that I will come back when the meal is over, and I trust a few hours' sleep will enable Her Imperial Majesty to see the Grand Duke of Hesse at least."

The Grand Duke Louis had succeeded to the title through his elder brother Alexander contracting a morganatic marriage, and the latter's son was Prince Alexander of Battenberg, now Bulgaria's ruler, so while one of these especially important visitors was the Tsarina's nephew, the other was her brother.

160

Kira knew the Grand Duchess Marie expected her to remain on duty the entire evening, but the Tsar had mentioned an opportunity for her to see her father. Then he expected the Tsarina to attend the banquet, but Count Chirnov was not invited because he did not belong to the Imperial family.

When a maid appeared with a supper tray for Kira, and her patient was still asleep, she asked how the banquet was progressing. According to the maid it had not yet begun, although timed to start three-quarters of an hour earlier, and the Imperial family remained in a drawing-room.

"It is said downstairs they are waiting for the Tsar, but he is still in his study with two very important princes, whose train arrived late," explained the woman.

Kira knew the Tsar could not be interrupted. She wondered where her father was waiting and asked the maid to find out. She intended then to get one of her fellow Maids of Honour to sit beside the Tsarina's bed for a quarter of an hour while she slipped out to see Count Chirnov.

But this never happened. The servant had only just left the room when Kira was thrown on the invalid's bed and for a moment lay there stunned. A deafening explosion shook the entire palace. Later she learnt it was loud enough to be heard as far as the north bank of the River Neva.

7

THE Tsarina remained in her drug-induced sleep. Kira managed to raise herself from the bed and feel for the floor with her feet, then stand up. The few dim lights in the room had gone out. She groped her way to a window and pulled back heavy velvet curtains. The explosion had not cracked the glass; outside glittered the illuminations already installed in Petersburg streets for the coming celebrations of Alexander II's twenty-fifth year as Tsar.

The door opened, admitting the Tsarina's personal maid and one of the nurses, both carrying lamps. Several members of the household were jealous of Kira because their mistress had taken such a fancy to her. Usually she was treated with frigid politeness that bordered on insolence, but tonight petty animosities vanished in terror and shock.

The nurse shrieked, "Those wicked Nihilists!"

Other attendants were crowding in, and Kira softly urged quiet so as not to disturb Her Majesty.

"Has she slept through it all?"

"Her Imperial Highness, the Grand-Duchess Marie, administered a morphine tablet, and mercifully she did not hear the explosion. Was it a bomb? Has anyone been killed?"

"A few servants and many guards were killed or injured."

"But the Tsar?"

"Praise be to Almighty God, the Tsar is unharmed."

"And the Imperial family has escaped."

Kira was about to ask more questions, but the Duchess appeared and the room emptied as if by magic. Kira remained standing attentively by the bed while the princess with a shaded candle bent over her mother and satisfied herself she was sleeping peacefully. Kira had never imagined the stiff Grand Duchess of Edinburgh could show such agitation, although she had realised the strong daughterly love. She was even more surprised to hear Marie of Edinburgh condescending to explain to a mere Maid of Honour what had happened.

A time bomb had been planted by Nihilists underneath the banqueting hall, though how they could have penetrated the strict security watch kept on all who worked at the Palace, seemed an impossibility. But there was a powerful bomb and it exploded about half an hour after the Imperial family should have sat down to dinner, the Tsar having ordered the meal to be served at six o'clock. He was usually fanatically punctual over such matters, but his programme was upset by lateness of the Grand Duke of Hesse's train so the Tsar was still closeted in his private study with nephew and brother-in-law. Nobody dared go to the study, nor could the meal be served without the imperial order, and the family waited in one of the drawing-rooms. Only the Tsarina was asleep upstairs, and not amongst them.

The explosion took place when the time was nearly half-past six. It was heard all over the great palace, but only the banqueting hall and the basement below it were wrecked, and people there killed or badly injured. Two butlers and eight footmen were in the banqueting hall and, consequently, victims.

"Then there were a number of officers and men belonging to the Finnish regiment, all assembled in the basement. I think it had been assigned as a waiting-room for those guards when not on actual duty."

The Grand Duchess spoke in an indifferent tone, not because she was by nature unkind, but upbringing and outlook were restricted. Obsessed with the majesty of tsardom, and her birth as daughter of Tsar Alexander II, she was incapable of considering any people below herself and her family as individuals worthy of consideration although as inferiors they must be treated kindly. They simply existed to serve. Unconsciously she had become fond of this new Maid of Honour who showed such devotion to her mother, but in the present moment of crisis it never occurred to her that Kira's personal feelings might be involved with the deaths of those who perished in the basement below the banqueting hall. And Kira was worried about her father.

Tsar Alexander II, broader and more humane than his daughter, had told her yesterday in front of the Grand Duchess that her father would be in the Winter Palace awaiting summons by the Prince of Bulgaria after the banquet. His words were clear in Kira's mind, "While we are dining, the Tsarina will have no need of your attendance, so there will be an opportunity for you and your father to be alone." But no such chance had occurred. The Tsarina was too ill to appear at the banquet. Kira remained on duty with Her Majesty. Count Chirnov was supposed to be in company with a former Finnish guard friend, as Kira learnt from an attendant who brought in a supper tray.

What had happened to Papa?

Kira waited in apprehension, but it was some time before the Grand Duchess dismissed her, saying one of the nurses must take over while she had some rest.

"You can be awakened immediately if Mama requires you."

Thankfully Kira escaped, but not to her own room. Instead she went to the floor below, saw the ghastly wreckage which was all that remained of the beautiful dining-hall, peered through broken floorage to equal chaos below, then was challenged by a soldier on guard. On learning who she was, the man took her to an officer from whom she learnt the names of those killed and injured. Hearing the shrieks of pain from some of the latter, she was almost glad to find Count Chirnov had been killed outright. She was taken to see his corpse. Dear, dear Papa! He was with Mama now, and he was at peace. Absurd at such a solemn moment she should reflect he could never carry out the mission the Tsar wanted him to undertake in Bulgaria. Who would help the Crown Prince in his difficulties now?

The Jubilee Celebrations must proceed, although the mourning Chirnov family would no longer take part in them. Police, Imperial family, even the Tsar himself, expecting to be assassinated as they drove through Petersburg in state, amid popular rejoicing on every side. Yes, all Russia appeared thankful for their ruler's escape from the Nihilist bomb planted within the stronghold of the Winter's Palace, but every precaution had apparently been taken then, as it was now. Yet, who could tell from where another blow might come?

Naturally the Winter Palace outrage was the subject of meticulous enquiries. They revealed cunning Nihilist planning combined with carelessness of those responsible for safety precautions. A few months previously some necessary structural repairs in the basement were begun, but although the credentials and passports of every workmen were checked, a certain Khaltourin, a secret Nihilist, deceived those responsible by his cleverly forged documents. Once working regularly amongst the other labourers, he contrived to get himself promoted to become foreman, then made love to a gendarme's daughter, and through her had access to an unknown hiding-place in the basement. Here he gradually collected material for his bomb, carrying in small sticks of dynamite in his pockets. Trained in bomb construction, he assembled one, equipped with a time device, and triggered to explode while the Tsar and other important Romanoffs were banqueting immediately above.

Khaltourin's scheme only failed in its object owing to the lateness of the train which caused lateness of the meal!

After this outrage, even Alexander II agreed to strict police precautions. When he drove through Petersburg streets, he was surrounded by soldiers and detectives, and he confined his drives to one of the parade grounds where he inspected troops, or to his eldest son's place. There was no private garden at the Winter Palace but the Anitchkov had an extensive one protected by high walls. Naturally Alexander could not take his mistress, so poor Princess Dolgoruky endured virtual imprisonment within her magnificent secluded suite of rooms. In the country, policing would be easier, her lover told her and promised to take her 'later on' to Tsarskoe Selo, or Peterhof, even the Crimea; but 'later on' meant after the death of the Tsarina who was slowly sinking under her consumptive complaint, though as yet it had not reached a critical stage. The Grand-Duchess Marie was obliged to return to England. The favourite, Kira, was to return after Count Chirnov's funeral because the Tsarina was so anxious to have her back in attendance.

Naturally the Chirnov family could not take part in the Jubilee Celebrations. Sergei, Lydia, and Kira accompanied the body of the late Count to the country estate, some fifty miles east of Moscow, where he was buried in the family vault next to his wife. It was etiquette for relatives to remain several months in mourning, withdrawing from all society. Sergei and Lydia had to submit to a custom they found irksome, while Kira would have been perfectly happy to enjoy the peace of Barona, but in her case imperial need would overrule custom, especially since there was no question of her appearing in public in Petersburg. She spent a fortnight at Barona after the funeral, and in that short time she saw a great deal more of her brother than she had ever done before. It surprised her to find Sergei took their father's death so lightly. He certainly did not miss Papa as she did. Kira tried not to be critical, but she was horrified to hear Sergei making plans for wringing more money out of the estate as soon as the obsequies ended. She knew little enough about her father's administration, yet Papa had been concerned about the peasants working for him and glad they were no longer serfs but free men. Now to hear Sergei and Lydia talk, Tsar Alexander II's decree for abolition of serfdom twenty years earlier might never have taken place.

The brother Kira had adored from childhood seemed to have changed into a totally different creature. The very day Count Chirnov's body was laid in the vault she met him with a strange-looking individual dressed in what she was certain was Jewish garb. Afterwards Sergei told her the man had followed him from Petersburg to claim payment of a debt.

"It is fine to be the Count at last. You don't realise how short of money I have always been." Sergei added the last sentence on seeing the shocked expression on her face.

"But you have your salary as a captain in the Preobrajenski and, in addition, Papa made you a personal allowance."

"Chicken-feed! The expensive life I

172

have been forced to lead in Petersburg has meant borrowing from Jewish moneylenders, and it has been a struggle to pay off their high rates of interest. Most of my friends are still in the same position, but now I have inherited Barona I shall be able to get out of debt in time."

"But Lydia had a huge fortune when you married her."

"I know, and that went. She wanted us to move in the best circles and crawl before the Tsarevich and Tsarevna. It all takes money. Still, you are all right, Kira. Papa has left you a generous portion. All the same, it behoves you to marry sensibly. The ideal husband for you is Hippolyte. Lydia made that very clear to you before the Anitchkov Palace reception, and during the short time we were there."

Sergei emphasised the words 'short time', but Kira made no comment. She did not want to have the subject of Prince Alexis revived. Memories hurt.

She changed the subject to that of their father, trying to rouse the proper sense of grief that Sergei must have, and she remarked on the esteem in which he was held by the Tsar.

"Look how His Imperial Majesty sent Papa on a special mission to Russian America, and would have done the same again to Bulgaria but for that Nihilist bomb. What was the mission in Bulgaria about?"

"The Tsarevna told Lydia it was a lot of nonsense. The Bulgars were helped by Russia to throw off the Turkish yoke, so Russia was asked to choose a ruler for them. They wanted a foreign prince. Well, they had none of their own. The Tsar chose his nephew, Prince Alexander of Battenberg, much to the Tsarevich's disgust since Prince Alexander was a military man without experience of government, but why the Tsar should think a senile old man like Papa would be of use in clearing up the mess . . . "

"Papa wasn't a senile old man!"

"He was senile enough to be taken in by Alexis Dolgoruky."

"You would not allow me to tell Papa about the duel and the card-cheating," retorted Kira. "Indeed he was not senile.

As for actual age, he was only a little older than the Tsar, and he was wise and shrewd. I am sure His Majesty will not find it easy to secure a substitute for this Bulgarian mission."

"If Alexander II has any sense he'll leave Bulgaria and Battenberg to sort out their problems. That is what the Tsarevich says."

"He is hardly a statesman — just a military-trained giant of great strength."

"Things will be different when he becomes Tsar Alexander III," remarked Sergei complacently.

It looked as though brother and sister were about to squabble for the first time in their lives, but there was an interruption by a servant who came to announce the arrival of Count Matvejevi. Kira was horrified at such bad taste in intruding on a family mourning, or what was supposed to be a family mourning, for Hippolyte was only a cousin of Lydia, not a Chirnov relative. Yet he was obviously expected. Sergei gave him an enthusiastic welcome, and sent word to Lydia who appeared, her black dress being her only concession to custom for her face was wreathed in smiles. She wanted news of their mutual wealthy aunt, whom he had been visiting in Moscow and was so old she was not expected to live much longer.

"Aunt Vera won't see another winter," declared Hippolyte.

Kira turned away in disgust. Lydia must have arranged her cousin's visit for the day after her father-in-law's burial, and Sergei had agreed. It pained Kira to see her brother so completely under his wife's influence. What was the matter with Sergei? Nothing could excuse such heartlessness, such disloyalty to their father. She kept contrasting the ensuing few days with the period of mourning kept by the late Count and herself for her mother. Papa had grieved, and that grief made him distant towards his daughter until the two came close together through acquaintance with Prince Alexis.

Then I displeased Papa through my refusal of the marriage offer, was her sad thought. But what else could she have done? Sergei ought to have allowed her to explain that Alexis was a man whose character she could not hold in respect.

Lack of respect killed love, or did it? Kira dared not dwell on the wonder of waltzing at the Anitchkov reception, but forced angry remembrance of that insulting kiss when she stated her reasons for refusing him. Yes, that kiss had been insulting! Her cheeks burnt with shame at the memory.

She was determined Hippolyte should not get the chance to kiss her, passionately or lightly. He lost no time in adopting a possessive attitude as if she was to be his second wife whether she consented or not. Lydia was eager for her to accept and made no secret of the fact. She was always arranging the couple be left together without either Sergei or herself present.

After this happened a few times, Kira turned on her would-be suitor.

"Don't talk as if we were betrothed. We are not and we are not likely to be. Nothing is further from my thoughts than marriage with my poor father just dead."

"Your father's death does not stop us being engaged. It is simply that you require Sergei's consent, not the late

Count Chirnov's, and Sergei wants you to become the Countess Matvejevi."

"That is something I cannot do."

"Look here, Kira Vassilievna, there is no time to lose. Lydia thinks the Tsarina will be sending for you any day. Then in spite of all this mourning fuss you will have to obey the imperial summons, but you shall go as my betrothed with marriage in view later on in the year."

"Thank you for the offer but my answer is no."

Hippolyte took no notice of this statement.

"Too bad you should have to be bothered with that sick Tsarina."

"I don't think so. I am fond of Her Imperial Majesty."

"You can't be. That Hessian princess has never been popular in Russia. People say she was so stiff and pious when she first came to the country. Then she was always organising charities. Then she lost her health — and her looks, I'll bet! No wonder the Tsar grew tired of her quickly."

In her turn Kira ignored Hippolyte's remarks. She said firmly, "Marriage is of no interest to me so you can not consider me your betrothed. And I am eager to return to serve the Tsarina."

"Well, you keep to the old woman's bedchamber and don't go amusing yourself in Petersburg."

"Amuse myself in Petersburg when I am in mourning!" exclaimed Kira indignantly.

"How thankful Sergei would be if some powerful person like the Tsarevich sent for him. He does hate rural life. He misses his *petites amies* from the *demi-monde*. Peasant women are not to his taste. They smell abominably. Besides, my dear cousin Lydia can watch him so easily, and he has no excuse of military duties."

"What do you mean?"

"Come, come, Kira Vassilievna, you are not such an innocent as that! Of course you understand me."

Kira did, and she declared hotly, "My brother is a model husband, and absolutely faithful to his wife. How dare you say otherwise! Of course he does not have a mistress."

"Not one mistress, my dear! Why, he is

known as one of the most noted libertines in Petersburg. But you need not think I am like that. I was no more unfaithful to my first wife than the Tsarevitch is to the Tsarevna, and I promise you that when we are married you shall have no cause to complain of my straying."

"We are not going to be married."

Kira rushed from the room. She was beside herself with rage, both at Hippolyte's calm assumption she was going to marry him, and at the accusations against Sergei. Of course he was not the kind of loose man depicted by Hippolyte. He could not be. It was impossible.

She gave orders for a horse to be saddled, then hurried to her room to change quickly into riding clothes. So anxious was she to get away from the house and sort out the confused ideas in her mind that she did not bother to ring her maid Anna.

Sergei unfaithful to his wife! Sergei a notorious libertine! No, she kept repeating to herself, but this short period of mourning at Barona had smeared the image of a wonderful brother. Sergei's absence of sorrow for their father's death, and his conception of this country estate as a mere source of money, shocked her intensely.

The movement of the horse eased some of the disgust that possessed her entire being. She let the creature go where he wished and he went across the snow-covered country taking the way to which he was most accustomed, namely, to the village. This was a collection of decent log huts which the late Count Chirnov had built to replace miserable ones unfit for human habitation. The sight of the new huts made Kira proud of her father's desire to benefit the peasants on his estate, but was followed by a conviction that Sergei would not have done so. Papa had also established a school and Kira guided the horse towards it. From behind the building came agonising shrieks. She saw a crowd gathered there when she pushed her way towards the sound.

Peasants stood in an orderly circle, as motionless as the statues in the Summer Garden and rendered indistinguishable by their padded winter garments. A few moved aside to make room for Kira and her horse so that she had an uninterrupted view of something she believed belonged to the days before Tsar Alexander II passed a decree abolishing serfdom. A man, wearing only a loin cloth although the cold was intense, stood, bound with rope to a post which he faced, while another man, whom Kira recognised as a farm overseer, flogged the victim's back with a cruel flail, its cutting wires covered with blood.

She heard Sergei's voice counting each stroke. Stupefied, she realised that this flogging was being carried out by her brother's orders, and the knowledge paralysed her. She sat in the saddle as passive as were the peasant spectators.

"Twenty-eight, twenty-nine, thirty!"

Sergei stopped. The overseer shook his whip, blood staining the snow, and handed it to a peasant in attendance. At a sign, others came forward, cut the rope around the body which fell to the ground. Yes, the man was dead. Sergei moved beside the corpse, took one look at it, then kicked it with his foot. A horse was led to him, and evidently he was told of Kira's presence, for he mounted and came up to her, seized her bridle, and they rode together through the village and in the direction of home.

"You ordered that flogging," stormed Kira. "How could you? Papa would never have acted so abominably."

But it was not the brother she thought she knew who replied.

"Now I am Count Chirnov I run Barona as I please. The whip is all these ignorant peasants can understand."

"It was a horrifying, barbaric scene!"

"Blame yourself for witnessing it."

"You have made me hate Barona."

Sergei laughed, a sneering contemptuous laugh.

"That is hardly a matter of concern for Lydia and me. You refuse to carry out our wishes in becoming betrothed to Hippolyte . . ."

"Indeed I do. I refuse to marry a man I do not love, and so far I have not met a man I can."

Was that true? Fortunately Sergei believed the lie as was shown by his scornful remarks about 'romantic female fools', and he accused her and her kind of not facing reality.

"And that will be your loss," he went on. "We know the Tsarina will be sending for you soon, and she will probably live for years in spite of the perpetual fuss about her health. Certainly you will be of age before she dies so I shall not be your guardian and you will have to shift for yourself. Papa left you a large enough fortune to keep you comfortably, even to pay some impoverished aristocrat to launch you in society, for, now you refuse to consider Hippolyte, Lydia is determined to wash her hands of you. You would be more suitable in a convent than in the fashionable world."

"I shall hire an elderly female companion, not an aristocrat, and we shall travel abroad."

"As you please. If you will not oblige Lydia and me by marrying Hippolyte, then we want nothing more to do with you."

The marriage of his sister to his wife's cousin was not so important to Sergei now he had this large inheritance. Before, he had needed a rich brother-in-law on whom to sponge, but now he could

184

pay off the money-lenders . . . Oh, do anything he wanted except avoid the prescribed period of mourning which chained him to Barona, even releasing him from his regiment so that he had no excuse for slipping back to Petersburg. How he envied Kira! The little bitch did not know how fortunate she was.

Later that evening a messenger arrived from Petersburg bearing an imposing letter sealed with the imperial crest of the double-headed eagle, and it contained a summons from the Tsar himself ordering Kira to resume her duties with the Tsarina. She need have no fear that official mourning for her father, the late Count Vassili Chirnov, would be disregarded. She would remain in seclusion at the Winter Palace. The Tsarina was too ill for society functions.

The Tsar had sent two sleighs, the first one hooded for Kira and her maid, as well as driver and groom, and pulled by three horses; the second carried two servants and baggage. Kira left Barona the next day with no feelings of regret. Her home was spoilt for her. She was sorry for the peasants and old family servants left behind, but thankful to have Anna, whom she had known all her life, for the woman had been personal maid to her mother. One did not have to pretend with Anna. Kira had already told her about the flogging and how Sergei's inflicting such a punishment horrified her. Anna too was disgusted and glad to return to Petersburg with her mistress, although she had hated the Winter Palace when she was there earlier. Each Maid of Honour was allowed a personal attendant.

Spring came late in Russia, and this month of March was part of deep winter, so travelling was done through snow, often very deep, and this made progress slower than in better conditions. There were four days of hard travelling before Petersburg was reached. However, days were lengthening, so in late afternoon the Winter Palace was suffused with sunshine and looking a more cheerful place than when Kira had left it.

Security seemed even stricter since the explosion that had wrecked the banqueting hall. Received by a high official, Kira was conducted through corridors heated by porcelain stoves to the imperial private apartments. Anna was taken to her mistress's bedchamber, with the baggage, while Kira was ushered into Her Majesty's boudoir.

The Tsarina smiled sweetly, stretched out a hand to be kissed, and said, "My dear child, I am so glad to have you back."

Kira had difficulty in restraining tears at such an affectionate welcome from the great lady. It was indeed a contrast to the coldness of Lydia and Sergei. Never mind the gloom of the Winter Palace, or monotony of attending a sick woman! Any happiness she could bring the dying Tsarina was a privilege, thought Kira, her eyes shining at the prospect of being wanted.

The weeks that followed were trying. April and May turned out to be unusually warm, but though the porcelain stoves had been let out it was too dangerous to open windows facing the Neva lest there came a shot from the opposite bank where an enemy, apparently part of the ordinary crowd, might be lurking.

An inner committee of the Nihilists, which Russia's Secret Police had been unable to detect, issued a declaration that political terrorism was a necessity and above all the Tsar was condemned to death by the movement. Once Alexander used to pride himself on moving freely and unattended about Petersburg, but after the Nihilist attempt to kill Princess Dolgoruky in the Summer Garden, then the narrow escape on the railway journey from the Crimea to Moscow, Alexander was forced to consider the safety measures advised by General Trepov. He hated going everywhere with guards, and at first tried not to permit this constant threat of death to alarm him. As far as possible he banished it from his mind but the explosion in the Winter Palace on the eve of his Jubilee Celebrations was too much to endure with equanimity. The asthma attacks he had suffered from childhood increased, taxing his strength. From being an erect man, seeming younger than his age, the Tsar looked old and nervous, and had even developed a slight stoop.

Anna, excluded like others from the third floor apartments, did discover that the Princess Dolgoruky and her children went in April to one of the palaces at the imperial country retreat of Tsarskoe Selo. The place was easily reached from Petersburg and considered easy to guard, also the road and railway running to it. Heavily protected, Kira heard that the Tsar paid two or three visits each week to his beloved mistress. His wife was now too weak to leave the Winter Palace, even to enjoy the high-walled large garden surrounding her eldest son's residence, although she sometimes talked of doing so and it was always 'tomorrow'. Pining as Kira was for outdoor exercise, she had no wish to take it in the grounds of the Anitchkov Palace. Memories of the reception there were too painful.

The Tsar's teasing behaviour that night was hardly believable when she watched the monarch making a duty visit to his ailing and still adoring wife. The first time he saw Kira he did briefly express sorrow over her father's death, but she sensed a coldness towards her, so different from his affability when visiting the Smolny. Of course he must have found out she had refused Prince Alexis's offer of marriage, and was interested because the Prince was really his son.

Kira felt he disapproved of her refusal. At least, that was the only way she could account for his behaviour that reminded her of her father's over the same matter.

If he had wanted her to marry Alexis, she supposed that was a great compliment. She wondered what the Princess Dolgoruky thought about it, for the Princess must be in her so-called brother's confidence. Over and over again, Kira recalled that visit to the mysterious third floor when Alexis took her to receive thanks for the Summer Garden incident. The Tsar too was very charming when he mentioned her action at the reception. He must have known who took her to visit his mistress, and from her, if not Alexis himself, he would learn that she, Kira Vassilievna Chirnov, had rejected a Dolgoruky by name but in reality the son of a Romanoff, Tsar Alexander II of all the Russias.

Could Alexis possibly be the villain Sergei insisted he was?

I ought to have listened to his account — his defence. Yes, I ought. If we could only meet again, I should ask him.

But there seemed no chance of that under present conditions. If Alexis came to the Winter Palace, the Maid of Honour nursing the Tsarina would not encounter him.

8

THE overpowering heat of this May made it harder for Kira to bear burdens. Last year she had the physical pleasure of riding most days in beautiful country that was bursting into life after a long hard winter. There was no joy of spring in the gloomy, stuffy Winter Palace, and though the Tsarina looked so extremely fragile, she gave the impression of a woman determined to cling to life as long as possible.

Further gossip informed Kira that the Tsar had moved to Tsarskoe Selo on medical advice, but he would be driving to Petersburg every day to attend to official business and see his wife, so the poor Tsarina expected a daily visit from him. Unable to tear himself away from Princess Dolgoruky, he was soon spending two or three nights in succession at Tsarskoe Selo.

A consolation came to the invalid through an unexpected visit from her daughter, the Grand Duchess Marie, who had been obliged to return to England after the Jubilee Celebrations. Now she was triumphant at having obtained Queen Victoria's permission to leave her small children — Alfred, Missy, Ducky and Sandra — with 'Grandma Queen' because her husband, an officer in the British Navy, was in the Baltic, and the ship scheduled to spend some time at the port of Kronstadt. He was able to take leave and escort his wife to Petersburg.

"I only wish you could have brought the children," sighed the Tsarina. Turning to Kira, she said, "Missy, that is Princess Marie, was so pretty when I last saw her. And Ducky was a lively little thing. They call me 'Grandmamma Empress', while their father's mother, Her Majesty, Queen Victoria, is 'Grandmamma Queen'. Ducky is named Victoria after her and has the second name of Melita because she was born on the island of Malta."

"Indeed, Ma'am," was Kira's dutiful response.

The Grand Duchess Marie was very affable to Kira, talking to her with far more warmth and less hauteur than she did to the other Maids of Honour.

"Her Imperial Majesty cannot speak highly enough of you."

"I am gratified to have pleased Her Imperial Majesty."

Prince Alfred, Duke of Edinburgh, was very bored and made no effort to conceal this. The Tsarina had fallen into a gentle doze when Kira heard him grumbling to his wife about the absence of Tsarevich and Tsarevna. With their children they had gone to their summer residence, which happened to be sixty miles south of Petersburg, so it was impossible for the Duke to visit during his short leave, especially as the Grand Duchess Marie disliked her sister-in-law, the Tsarevna. She was jealous of the former Danish princess's charm and Prince Alfred's praise irritated her.

"Not that I mind missing Sasha. Such a dull ponderous fellow! And I am not interested in his feats of strength. But Minnie is vivacious, like Alex — well, more so because she is witty and poor Alex does not hear half one's jokes because of her deafness."

Minnie was the pet name of the Tsarevna, who had been Princess Dagmar of Denmark before marriage, while her sister, Princess Alexandra, was now Princess of Wales, wife of the Duke's elder brother.

"Go for a day's drive to Tsarskoe Selo."

"You sent a message to your father that you were here and he said he would come the day after tomorrow, so there is no need for me to chase over to Tsarskoe Selo. As a matter of fact there is a famous observatory I have never seen, and to a naval officer like me, its instruments and its work generally are of interest. You know how I like Greenwich, and this Pulkova is of the same importance. I've been enquiring and the place is only ten miles away."

Prince Alfred wanted to see instruments used in the observatory, not bother with stargazing, so had no need to spend a night there. The Tsarina woke up and heard the end of his plan. Always anxious to please, she declared Affie must take her daughter with him.

"You both need a day out, driving in

195

an open carriage in order to enjoy our fine Russian country air. Yes, Marie, I insist. You have never been to Pulkova, have you?"

"No, but nor have you, Mama."

"My visit must wait," said the Tsarina bravely, though she and her listeners knew she would never be fit to go. Even Tsarskoe Selo was beyond her powers, and with two imperial palaces there she need not have occupied the same one as her rival.

"But, Mama, I cannot bear to leave you for a whole day."

"Affie will enjoy the outing much more if you accompany him. Of course you must go, dear."

The Grand Duchess wavered. Then she said, "I am sure Kira Vassilievna will look after you properly, Mama."

By nature the Tsarina Marie was a very unselfish woman, nor was she so obsessed with her exalted position as her daughter. She turned in her chair to glance at the Maid of Honour standing behind, and noted the white face and the dark shadows beneath Kira's eyes.

"I have three other Maids of Honour

to entertain me. Kira Vassilievna looks as if she needs a day in the country, so let her accompany you and Affie. It is impossible for you two to ride alone in an open carriage because His Majesty has left security precautions in the hands of General Trepov, so the General or another high-ranking Secret Police official will have to sit with you. Of course you will have an escort of armed Cossacks as well."

The Duke of Edinburgh was too well trained in naval obedience to dispute any command laid down by the Tsar, and a well protected carriage left the Winter Palace next morning. General Trepov did not come but sent a certain Colonel Danilsov, a trim officer whom Kira judged to be about the same age as Sergei, or even Prince Alexis.

She had ample time to recall her former journey to Pulkova with Alexis and her father. What a contrast in every way! Then it had been winter, but the sunshine was gentle and benign instead of fiercely scorching. Snow lay everywhere, whereas now grass and flowers, even trees, had a dried-up appearance. Dear Papa had talked about astronomy to Alexis, who dutifully answered his questions, but still found time to smile at Kira sitting beside him in the swift-moving sledge. Today the carriage proceeded at a brisk pace, only its occupants were silent. The Grand Duchess liked stimulating discussions with those she considered her equal, or nearly her equal, and today that category embraced only her husband. Kira was unaware that the Duke of Edinburgh was known among intimates to be an unusually silent man who disliked obligation to take part in conversation, even with his wife.

Opposite the royal couple sat Kira and the Secret Service official responsible for their safety. He was a fair-complexioned man with sandy hair and short beard. Kira decided he would be pleasant off-duty, but in his capacity as representative of the Third Section, the general name for the Secret Service — she found him a dull travelling companion. In any case, they could not have chatted in the royal couple's presence.

So Kira surveyed the scenery, trying to suppress pangs of anguish. Within herself she argued that it was absurd to cherish feelings of remorse for her rejection of Alexis. What else could she have done, although now she realised she had been in love with him — even perhaps on their visit to Pulkova? And she still was, in spite of knowing his unworthiness.

She believed all Sergei said, yet doubt had arisen in her mind since staying at Barona with him as the Count Chirnov. That period, short as it was, killed her former faith in the perfect brother. Although she had adored Sergei from childhood, she at last acknowledged the truth of Prince Alexis's remark, "Your lives have gone along different lines." He meant that the greater part of her brother's life was unknown to her, which was perfectly true. Sergei was many years older, and they had been totally separated during the years she was in Russian America and in northern Greece.

Until recently she was ignorant of his real character, a character that was greatly at fault in his financial recklessness, also lack of filial affection, and perhaps in adherence to the strict truth. Not that she had reached the stage of doubting his veracity concerning Alexis and the card cheating, nor the duel in which he acted as second to Prince Ivan Granovski, but could there have been some extenuating circumstances as well?

Back came the monotonous reproach that she had acted wrongly in not listening to what Alexis was anxious to tell her. She grew hot at the memory of refusing to give him a hearing. He had been so confident she would do that.

Then came the brutal kiss. It was shameful behaviour on his part, she told herself, yet she knew she would have given anything to receive another kiss.

Repressing such a shocking desire, she began to weave hopes on today's meeting, for surely he would be on duty at Pulkova. The Director of the Observatory, Herr Struve, would attend the Duke and Duchess of Edinburgh, and possibly Prince Alexis would escort herself and Colonel Danilsov. Somehow she must contrive to speak privately with Alexis, though she had no idea what to say beyond making an apology for her previous refusal to grant him a hearing.

If only these mists could be cleared

away! Wicked though it might be to want him again, to want a renewal of his former attentions, yet Kira acknowledged that she did, whether he were worthy of her love or not.

The silver domes came into sight, shining brilliantly in the strong sunlight. Instead of a snow-covered landscape, the country round the Observatory was bright with flowers, like daisies and dandelions, growing amid coarse grass that had already lost its fresh spring greenness. When the carriage stopped in front of the entrance portico, Kira was quivering with excitement. Yes, he was there, standing behind Herr Struve. Thank God he had not gone to Petersburg to make a routine report. He was here at Pulkova, and she, Kira Vassilievna, was going to repair her previous harsh blunder of condemning him unheard.

After the distinguished visitors were received by Herr Struve, then surely Prince Alexis would be presented. It suddenly struck Kira that the name Dolgoruky must grate unpleasantly on the Grand Duchess's ears, since it revealed kinship with her father's mistress. Kira had heard she refused to join the Tsarevich and other brothers in condemning the Tsar's behaviour with its insult to their mother. Marie ignored the affair, but in deference to the Tsarina she had nothing to do with the Princess Catherine or any other members of the Dolgoruky family.

As for Prince Alexis being her father's illegitimate son, she was unlikely to be aware of that.

Herr Struve's bow was respectfully low as he received the exalted couple. The Duke of Edinburgh immediately changed from silence to loquacity as he showed off his knowledge of the famous Observatory before being taken to inspect it. His wife saw no reason to introduce her mother's Maid of Honour, while the Third Section official was ignored, and Herr Struve was too overawed to notice or he would have recognised Kira.

She walked with Colonel Danilsov several paces behind the Duke and Duchess of Edinburgh, and naturally Prince Alexis came with them. He gave Kira a slight bow when she greeted him, then expressed formal condolences on her father's death; but did not even wait for formal thanks before warmly expressing delight in meeting the Colonel whom he addressed as Boris. Apparently they were old friends, for Colonel Danilsov addressed him as Alexis.

Kira felt herself to be superfluous, and she did not like it, but under the circumstances it was impossible to leave the two men. She could not join the Edinburgh couple and Herr Struve, nor could she deliberately wander about the Observatory on her own. She had to remain with Alexis and Colonel Danilsov, listening to their conversation about acquaintances and places of which she knew nothing.

The behaviour of Alexis chagrined her. His icy indifference killed all hope of apologising for her former hardness. There was no opportunity to tell him she was prepared to listen to any explanation he could give that mitigated the accusations made by Sergei, and by now she was certain he was not the despicable villain as branded by her brother. Disillusionment with Sergei brought about doubts. Moreover, she knew now that, willingly or unwillingly, she was in love with Alexis, and dread seized her that her rejection had killed the love he once expressed for her. Beyond a frigidly polite reference to her father's death, he ignored her.

In turn he was being ignored by the Grand Duchess. Herr Struve presented him to her and to Prince Alfred. The name Dolgoruky did not appear to have any significance for the Duke of Edinburgh, who was too engrossed in the Observatory's wonders to be interested in individuals, but Kira noted the look on his wife's face and the haughty indifference directed at this other astronomer. Immediately she turned to Herr Struve, asking where was the portrait of His Imperial Majesty, Tsar Nicholas I, who had founded the institution.

Prince Alfred waved aside an offer of refreshments. Time enough for them when he had viewed the Observatory, and as the tour began he talked authoritatively to Herr Struve about the one at Greenwich in England.

"Of course you are acquainted with Greenwich," remarked Colonel Danilsov to Alexis.

"Yes, very well."

"And is astronomy still the first priority in your life?"

"Not merely first but the only one," came the almost fierce reply. "The magnitude of the heavens and the innumerable objects which make an astronomer realise the unimportance of planet Earth . . . "

"Be careful, Alexis. What you are saying could be misinterpreted as challenging the teachings of the Orthodox Church."

"I had no such intention. As an official in the Secret Third Section, Boris, you are over-cautious. Oh, our Tsar is a liberal-minded person, but I know that not all surrounding him are, and a remark uttered in innocence and repeated in equal innocence . . . "

Here Kira struck in. She could remain silent no longer.

"I suspect you two gentlemen are fearful I might speak unguardedly to my brother, Captain Count Chirnov, though he has left the army on inheriting our father's estates. And he and my sister-in-law are intimate with the Tsarevich and Tsarevna. But, Colonel Danilsov, I would not repeat anything you and His Highness Prince Alexis might say. I am no meddler. Being a Maid of Honour to the Tsarina has taught me discretion if I did not know its value before."

She paused a minute, then continued, "My father was interested in facts His Highness Prince Alexis gave him concerning stars and galaxies, but my brother's tastes do not lie in that direction."

Kira was hoping Alexis would say something about her curiosity, even recall how he had shown her planet Jupiter through the big telescope, but instead he gave a scornful laugh.

"So, my dear Boris," he declared, "you need not worry that I am qualifying for the Vladimir Highway."

"Where is the Vladimir Highway?" asked Kira, determined not to be excluded from conversation between these two any longer.

"It is a common term for the route taken by convicts when marching to

Siberia," replied Colonel Danilsov.

He seemed to be finding the trio and the general conversation embarrassing, and made a pretence of listening to the loud-toned explanations given to the royal couple by Herr Struve. Kira felt as if all hope were dying within her. Alexis must be deliberately trying to hurt her through his aloofness — yes, he was paying her back for the way she had behaved to him when they last met. He no longer had any love for her so he was enjoying revenge.

But that maddening passionate kiss he gave her when they parted last! Recalling it now, she acknowledged that it had been a kiss turning her from schoolgirl into young woman, a kiss that gave her a glimpse of what love could really mean.

As the party passed into the next room, she heard him telling Colonel Danilsov he had not been in Petersburg since February, but when he came next they must dine at the Gribodskaya, which Kira concluded to be a fashionable restaurant. She wished females were not debarred from going about freely and patronising the capital's spectacular haunts, but had as much liberty as men.

On leaving the second room they had a narrow iron staircase to ascend, and here Kira pretended to have difficulty, a trick she hoped might rouse Alexis to gallantry, especially as he was immediately behind, but he did nothing and it was Colonel Danilsov who pushed in front of Alexis, saying, "Let me assist you."

They reached the library, where the Duke of Edinburgh showed signs of boredom and an eagerness to get to the telescope. Mention of the instrument brought anguish to Kira when she remembered her previous visit and the trouble Alexis had taken to explain its wonders. However, there was a delay because the Grand Duchess Marie lingered over the portrait of Tsar Nicholas I, which hung in the library and boasted about her grandfather's achievements.

If only I could manage to have a word alone with Alexis, sighed Kira. She was by now sure Sergei had made a mistake over the card-cheating; since, if Alexis had really been a swindler, would a man in Colonel Danilsov's position be so friendly with a man guilty of such behaviour, and the two were undeniably friends.

Prince Alfred began to ask questions about the telescope as soon as they came to it, but his wife showed her boredom and engaged Herr Struve in conversation, so Alexis was called to attend to the royal Duke. Thus Kira and Colonel Danilsov were left standing in the background.

Surveying her closely, Boris Danilsov could see this Maid of Honour was on the verge of tears, and wondered why she was so obviously upset. It was easy to hazard a guess. He had noticed the way her eyes had been following Prince Alexis, and the revelation of her father's interest in astronomy implied previous acquaintance, but there must have been a quarrel. Otherwise why was Alexis treating her with such disdain? However, curiosity was tempered by the caution planted in him by secret police training. He made no attempt to uncover the mystery, but welcomed Kira herself asking a question when she had to get her emotions under control.

"I gather, Colonel, that you and His Highness, the Prince Alexis Dolgoruky,

209

are friends of long standing?"

He laughed and replied, "Yes, Mademoiselle. From cadet school, where we started our military training, into the Preobrajenski regiment together, and we have kept in touch since we left. Prince Alexis wanted to pursue a university study of science and mathematics which became astronomy, while I continued a soldier until I was selected for other work."

"What is called the Third Section?"

Again he smiled.

"Officers who show — shall we say! — a certain talent are transferred to the Police. I do not think I was cut out for the Army. My present duties are far more interesting."

But Kira was anxious to probe into his Preobrajenski days.

"Sergei, my brother, was in the Preobrajenski. You must have known him. He recently resigned because my father's death gave him estates to care for, and he is now Count Chirnov."

The Colonel bowed. Although Kira did not realise it, he found the thought of Sergei Chirnov in the role of model estate owner distinctly ludicrous.

"You must also have known my sister-in-law's brother, the late Prince Ivan Granovski."

Another bow of assent. Kira grew bolder.

"Sergei told me he acted as second for Prince Ivan who — against rules — fought a duel with Prince Alexis. Did you know about this duel? The participants nearly got expelled."

She dared not say Alexis did suffer expulsion.

"I acted as second to my friend Prince Alexis" came the astonishing reply. Then he must know the truth! Only what was the truth? A man who had risen to a high position in the Third Section would not in his younger days have given support to a card-cheat, and seconds in a duel were supporting the combatants.

"If Your Imperial Highness will condescend to partake of refreshments . . . "

Herr Struve's voice boomed through the room. The Grand Duchess, weary of everything connected with stars, was glad to have something to eat and moved forward with alacrity. Her husband followed. He had exhausted his investigations so was satisfied, and Kira saw the telescope being lowered, also the covering for part of the silver dome moving over the aperture. Inwardly rebellious, she followed the Edinburghs and Herr Struve, conscious that she had lost her chance of questioning Colonel Danilsov any further. She was not put next to him at the meal. Two astronomers sat on either side of her, one being Alexis who ignored her completely, and she just dared not speak to him or she would have burst into tears. It was a relief when the carriage was announced.

Herr Struve did notice her then and referred to Count Chirnov's visit with her, then offered sympathies when Kira explained he had been killed in the Winter Palace explosion. No more could be said. The Grand Duchess Marie was impatient to leave. She reproved her husband for asking further questions.

"You know I want to hasten back to Mama."

The Duke followed his wife into the carriage quite meekly. Herr Struve handed in Kira. Alexis did not attempt to bid her good day, but drew back for his Third Section friend to take the remaining seat. Prince Alfred of Edinburgh, for whom the name Dolgoruky evidently had no significance, gave a few words of praise to 'the astronomer who showed me the telescope' and congratulated Herr Struve on having such a clever member of staff.

"Alas, I am going to lose him, Your Royal Highness," said the Director. "His Imperial Majesty the Tsar has plans to send Prince Alexis abroad."

"Oh, His Majesty must not do that. I shall have a few words with him."

The carriage moved off with the Grand Duchess Marie saying in a low tone to her husband, but not so low that Kira did not hear it.

"You cannot interfere with Papa's arrangements. We will have a talk later about the — er — implications. You do not know who Prince Alexis is but I do. No more now!"

Of course the daughter of the injured Tsarina would hate all the Dolgoruky family, and there was also the secret relationship to her father, but none of that affected Sergei's accusations. Hurt and miserable, Kira watched the silver domes of Pulkova recede from view. She never wanted to see the Observatory again, and if Alexis was going abroad . . . oh, it was the end of everything for her!

Whether he is a card-cheater or not . . . no, he is not now, and even if he once was, I love him. He is the only man I can ever love.

The thought clung to her as the carriage covered the ten miles to Petersburg, and so obsessed was she with imagining her miserable future that she paid no attention to the scenery and was amazed when they stopped at the main entrance of the Winter Palace. But as Kira followed the Duchess and Duke inside she was struck by the atmosphere of tragedy which met them.

"How is Her Imperial Majesty?" asked Grand Duchess Marie.

Very ill. Extreme unction was being administered. Word had been sent to His Imperial Majesty at Tsarskoe Selo.

The sick unhappy Tsarina was dying.

9

THE night passed slowly. Dawn came, but still the Tsarina lingered. Most of the time she was in a coma, only occasionally her eyes opened for a moment as if hoping to see her husband bending over her. Her sons had arrived and were in the bedchamber, with her daughter. The Tsarevich and his wife had travelled four times the distance between Petersburg and Tsarskoe Selo, so the Tsar should have come hours ago.

So thought Kira, wearied through lack of sleep but obliged to remain on duty with the other Maids of Honour, all standing in the background.

The Grand Duchess Marie sat close to her mother, holding one of the feeble hands. At the foot of the bed, supported by priests in gorgeous vestments and holding up lighted wax tapers to illuminate it, was a huge case of ikons, or sacred pictures. They were of great importance in the Russian Orthodox rites. The bedchamber was also filled by more members of the Imperial family, more clergy, doctors, and attendants like the superfluous Maids of Honour.

This was the end of a life that had lasted fifty-seven years, and had been a life of great happiness and great misery.

A situation had arisen that was common in the aristocratic circles of Petersburg. Men continued to cohabit with their wives but also sought other female distractions, and the wives treated them lovingly and ignored these extramarital infidelities. Marie of Hesse had followed this custom, but she suffered inwardly through her great love for Alexander, and subsequent confinements damaged her health. The birth of her last child, the Grand Duke Paul, left her a complete invalid. She was obliged to make frequent trips to German spas for treatment, then spend winters in a less severe climate than that of Petersburg. When she was in the capital she was often too unwell to carry out state social duties. Alexander grew increasingly bored with her.

He had a succession of ephemeral mistresses but there was a difference when he fell in love with Princess Catherine Dolgoruky, now eighteen. She resisted his advances for a year, then capitulated. For more than a decade she had been the Tsar's mistress and he was absolutely faithful to her. Poor Tsarina Marie had long abandoned any hope of Catherine being discarded. In fact, she guessed that when she died, Alexander would marry the woman who had supplanted her.

Perhaps that was why she fought off death during the night and early morning, but at eight o'clock she ceased to make the effort and passed away. The chief physician solemnly pronounced the words, "Her Imperial Majesty is no more." Priests moved closer together in order to make way for each member of the Imperial family to advance and kiss a lifeless hand. Of course Kira just stood in the background waiting until the room began to empty. As she left, there were only priests holding lighted tapers and chanting prayers, while in a corner waited a group of attendants. From her mother's death, she knew their function was to prepare the body for burial.

Still there was no sign of the Tsar.

The Maids of Honour were told they could retire to rest for the remainder of the day. This information was given in the late Tsarina's boudoir where all who left the chamber of death were having refreshments. Kira drank a cup of freshly made hot tea that took away a little of her tiredness, but she could not eat. She grieved for her former mistress who had been exceptionally kind to her and of whom she had grown very fond.

Her own future depressed her. At Barona Sergei foresaw the Tsarina living much longer and retaining Kira as a Maid of Honour, so that he would have no need to exercise guardian rights. But with the Tsarina's death Kira would not legally come of age for two years, and during that time brother and sister-in-law could compel her to live with them, even if they could not force her into marriage with Hippolyte against her wish. Not that Hippolyte worried her now. She felt her determination to refuse him had really penetrated before she left Barona. His goodbye had been cold enough to show he was offended. She had no doubt he would seek a more amiable lady now she was out of the way.

What had shocked her were the things he said about Sergei, revelations she feared were true, or partly true, since she herself had discovered he was different from the fine brother she thought he was. To live with him and Lydia would be horrible! She had no affection for either, whereas she had grown to love the dead Tsarina.

But I cannot mourn for her because I am glad she is at peace, thought Kira.

Her strained nerves craved solitude, and to avoid the other three Maids of Honour, she slipped out of the boudoir unobtrusively; but before she reached her bedchamber, where the faithful Anna would be waiting up for her, an unaccountable restlessness came over Kira. In spite of safety precautions, the corridor leading to rooms set aside for members of the late Tsarina's entourage was empty of sentries. Kira ran down one of the many staircases to the floor below and found a modicum of calm as she wandered through several empty halls, the morning light showing their painted ceilings and malachite pillars;

219

although the valuable furniture, statues and carpets were shrouded in dust covers while not used for entertaining. With a mind occupied by sad thoughts, she was hardly conscious of her surroundings until she was roused by reaching the main entrance hall of the palace. Here stood numerous footmen, all at attention and facing the front door. Kira was just able to slip behind a pillar without being noticed as the Tsar arrived.

So he had come at last, but he was not alone. With him, of all people, was Prince Alexis.

She saw the two mount the great principal marble staircase. In accordance with rank, Alexis was three steps behind. Guards followed while the footmen disappeared as if by magic. Seeing the vast hall empty, Kira left her pillar and began to creep up the same staircase, realising she must get to the next floor where her bedchamber was. The presence of Alexis puzzled her. Surely he took no share in mourning for the Tsarina, so he must be going to the third floor where his supposed sister had her private suite.

Hiding behind another pillar after

leaving the staircase, in a high upper hall, she saw the two men separate. Alexis bowed and kissed his father's hand, while the Tsar, followed by guards, walked along a corridor which Kira knew led to the private Imperial apartments. Alexis waited a minute then took the opposite direction. Nobody else was about. Kira hurried in pursuit, was in time to see him take another turning, then another staircase. She was certain now he must be making for Princess Dolgoruky's apartments, but hoped to attract his attention before he reached the guarded entrance. No, it could not be the one where there was a lift; her sense of direction was clear.

What she did not know was that Alexis had a couple of rooms for his personal use, and that they were in a remote wing with easy access to a side entrance. Alexis had his own keys, and though every entrance was guarded by sentries, none challenged him. His visits to Petersburg were infrequent, but he was well-known to those responsible for security as a favourite of the Tsar. Officially he was the Princess Dolgoruky's brother. That he was a son of Alexander II was also suspected. In any case he was classified as reliable.

On top of the staircase Alexis took to the third floor, Kira was stopped by a sentry suddenly emerging from his guard position.

"Please let me pass. I must speak with Prince Alexis Dolgoruky. It is very important."

Her voice rang out in desperation, and though Alexis was some distance ahead it reached him and he turned round. With pride in shreds, Kira called to him.

"I have something important to say to you, Highness."

She heard her own voice, thin and quavering, say in addition, "There was no opportunity at Pulkova yesterday."

Could it have been only yesterday, less than twenty-four hours ago?

She was still standing on the second step from the top of the staircase as Alexis dismissed the sentry with a flick of his finger in true imperial fashion. With the man withdrawn, he came to the top, looking down on Kira. His manner was cold and imperious, as one might expect from a son of Tsar Alexander II, although that son was unacknowledged.

"My private apartments are at the end of this corridor, but it would hardly be seemly to invite you in when unchaperoned, so I am sorry to keep you standing here while you state what you wish to say to me."

Oh, he was stiff and infuriating! She could not abase herself by apologising for her previous injustice for being unjust in refusing to hear his side of the card-cheating and duel — that was how she had offended him, but Sergei had said . . .

"Well, Mademoiselle, how can I be of service to you?"

Rather feebly she said, "The Tsarina has just expired."

"So His Imperial Majesty was informed on arrival. News that she was on the point of death reached him at Pulkova by dawn this morning. The messenger had first gone to Tsarskoe Selo."

"But was not His Majesty staying at Tsarskoe Selo?"

"He was, but came to Pulkova to see me on a private matter. On hearing of

223

the Duke and Duchess of Edinburgh's visit, he did not wish to encounter them so remained in the seclusion of the Director's residence until their departure. I rely on you not to speak of the matter, though it hardly comes under the category of state secret, and Herr Struve was somewhat indiscreet in revealing His Majesty's plan to send me abroad. There was no reason for him to tell the Duke of Edinburgh that."

Alexis stopped awkwardly, as if he wanted to say more, to speak on the old friendly terms, yet memories of that final acrimonious scene kept up a barrier.

Kira shamelessly asked, "Where are you going?"

"To Bulgaria. Important people like the Tsarevich will be acquainted with that before today ends. I start in a couple of hours, and nothing is a true secret in this Winter Palace hotbed of gossip."

"But why are you being sent to Bulgaria? Is there an observatory there? I thought it was a very primitive country."

Alexis actually smiled.

"You are right, but His Majesty

requires me to suspend my astronomical work for a short period and assist the Crown Prince in certain matters of interest in Russia. In fact, I am to undertake the task which was to have been your father's. That is, a diplomatic mission, and I, alas, am not experienced in such work as he was. Again, Mademoiselle, I express my deepest sympathy with you over his tragic death."

"Thank you," came Kira's mechanical response.

Naturally the Tsarina had meant nothing to him, but grief over her passing and the general weariness of so many hours' vigil was badly affecting Kira. Alexis could perceive she was looking physically exhausted. He enquired if she could find her way to the apartments occupied by Maids of Honour, admitting his knowledge of the palace interior was somewhat limited. So should he summon a servant to conduct her?

It was now or never!

"There is something I wish to say to you."

"At your service, Mademoiselle Chirnov."

The polite phrase was pregnant with unwillingness to serve her. The mode of address was like having a piece of ice thrown in one's face. If he would only call her Kira Vassilievna again!

"It is not that I discount my brother's revelations about card-cheating and a duel, but I apologise for not permitting you . . . " She could hardly say 'Give your version of the affair.' Brokenly she went on, " . . . not hearing you. I mean, perhaps there were extenuating circumstances of which Sergei was unaware."

At this unexpected remark, Alex was certainly staggered. He was overwhelmed by a desire to tell Kira the entire truth, but how could he when she believed implicitly in that dastardly brother of hers? Hopeless! He must forget he had ever cared. Since she accepted Sergei as a being incapable of deceit, nothing would alter her fundamental prejudice.

"You are generous, Mademoiselle, but the facts remain the same. I was accused of a crime on account of which I fought a duel. One cannot undo the past."

Alexis was surprised by the wistful look on Kira's face. Her manner, too was so different from that when she stubbornly refused to listen to him on a previous occasion.

She said, "A past can be put aside. I am sure, however wrongly you acted all those years ago, you would not behave in the same way again."

"You are being very charitable, Mademoiselle," was all he could say, at the same time obsessed by the uselessness of making any confidence. He could guess what Sergei had said about him. Kira too remembered her brother's convincing accusations, but since hearing them she had been horrified by the new Count Chirnov's harshness, even cruelty, to the peasants at Barona. Her father regarded them as human beings. They were required to work for him at low wages, but better living conditions and education were essential, while he endeavoured to abolish flogging, certainly restrict its use. To Sergei the peasants were still serfs, property he could exploit and flog to death if need be. That awful scene she had witnessed came back to her. For the moment she thought Alexis's card-cheating was a minor offence compared with Sergei's brutishness.

The silence was broken by a voice she recognised. It was calling, "Your Highness, I have been searching everywhere for you. Oh, I beg your pardon, Prince!"

Striding towards them was Colonel Danilsov. He had seen Alexis from the far end of the corridor, but not Kira. Standing on the staircase she had been hidden by her companion.

"Mademoiselle Chirnov lost her way, Boris. I was about to summon a guard to conduct her to her apartment which is situated among others belonging to the Tsarina's entourage. Of course I mean the late Tsarina! My knowledge of this palace is confined to a couple of apartments allotted to me by the Tsar for my personal use, and to my sister's private suite. I rarely go below the third floor. Only when His Majesty summons me to his private study. This morning I returned from Pulkova in company with him."

He is taking a lot of trouble to explain, thought Kira, and her heart sank further as she realised he could dwell on such petty details while ignoring her. There was no hope of ever reviving his love.

Colonel Boris Danilsov was looking embarrassed. Unwittingly he had interrupted a private conversation that might have led to something. That was how Boris expressed it. He had observed enough at Pulkova to guess there was love on Kira's side, but he could not understand Alexis. Anyway, with the latter on the point of departing for Bulgaria, there was no hope of anything definite between the couple.

A hurt Kira retreated into her shell. With cold dignity she said she should be obliged if a servant were called to show her to the Maids of Honour's bedchambers. As it was she was completely lost, never having been in this part of the palace before.

A servant came to conduct her. Hardly daring to glance at Alexis lest she should betray her emotions, and anxious to escape even a polite kissing of hands, Kira curtly bade good day to both men and hurried away. The meeting had been such agony that she could be thankful he was going to Bulgaria.

A lesser cause of distress was what would be her own future in the interval that must still elapse before she came of age. Surely Sergei and Lydia would not want her to live with them! She naturally expected to continue as Maid of Honour — without duties — until the funeral rites for the late Tsarina ended. The usual period for these was a month, so, like everybody else, Kira was surprised at the almost indecent haste shown by the Tsar in compressing the obsequies into a single week.

The Tsarevich and Tsarevna said a great deal behind the monarch's back that they dared not do to his face. It was the same with the other Grand Dukes and their wives, but the Grand Duchess Marie, although shocked, refused to listen to criticism of her father. She and her husband had a private quarrel on the subject, and she was scarcely on speaking terms with her brothers.

Isolation was depressing at such a time of grief, and in spite of her pride in being a Grand Duchess of Russia, she singled out the Maid of Honour for whom her mother had shown such fondness. With a

230

consideration rare in her, Marie actually noticed Kira's pallor.

"You look worn-out, Kira Vassilievna," she remarked. "You will be glad to finish at Court and go into the country. I understand there is a family estate now belonging to your brother."

Something in the flat unenthusiasm of Kira's reply urged Marie to probe further, and she gathered Barona would not be a happy retreat because the tragedy of three months ago was still foremost in the girl's mind. Of course, the late Count Chirnov lost his life in that dreadful Nihilist explosion at the Winter Palace. Papa had been deeply concerned over the loss of a man he esteemed so highly.

Acting on a sudden impulse, a rare thing in her, Marie invited Kira to accompany her back to England, saying the change of scene would do her good and that she must stay for a long time.

"Certainly until the autumn because I shall not be going into society for a few months. Queen Victoria, my mother-in-law, will understand the need for me to show proper respect to my own dear mother's memory."

This suited Kira, who had no desire at present for gaieties. She guessed she would be expected to be an unpaid companion to the Grand Duchess Marie, not a guest to be treated as an equal. And she admired the Duchess of Edinburgh's loyalty to both parents. Hauteur could be excused when there was also evidence of kindness.

A daughter of Tsar Alexander did not condescend to write to Sergei, asking that guardian's permission to permit his sister to stay with her in England. She put her request before the Tsar, who gave the imperial permission, adding that the present Count Chirnov would be informed "by a letter from one of my secretaries and signed by me."

"Do you think as highly of the son as you did of the father?"

"Heavens, No! Sergei Vassilievich is no son of which any father could be proud. I only trust his father died without full knowledge of his depravity. Marriage was his best achievement. His wife was a Granovski, and she is a great favourite of Sasha and Dagmar. I was glad for the daughter Kira to be placed among your mother's Maids of Honour. I am glad you wish to take her to England."

"Mama showed her great favour."

The Tsar stiffened uncomfortably. He knew he was behaving abominably in hurrying up the burial of his late wife, but a week of pretended grief was the utmost he felt he could endure. He was so anxious to make the woman he loved his wife and legitimise their three children.

Regarding Kira, although he was annoyed with the girl, sensing she had made Alexis unhappy, yet he was grateful to her for saving Catherine's life in the Summer Garden. Her departure for England with Marie was the best immediate course. He had other plans later.

When I openly proclaim Catherine as Tsarina, then I shall send for Kira Vassilievna, for she will make a loyal Maid of Honour to my darling, and maybe, when Alexis finishes in Bulgaria, that affair may be patched up.

Besides being thankful for a temporary escape from Sergei and Lydia, Kira was delighted with the beauty of England,

and could not understand why the Grand Duchess Marie was always comparing it unfavourably with Russia. They went first to London where the Edinburghs lived at Clarence House, a handsome mansion overlooking a beautiful thoroughfare called the Mall. Then they went to the country, and here the Grand Duchess intended to remain until out of mourning. Kira had no objection to the arrangements because she cared nothing for London Society, whether she were a part of it or not, but she did wonder what would happen to her after the Duchess resumed English Court life. She liked the Edinburgh estate of Eastwell Park in Kent and thought the countryside gentler and pleasanter than around Barona, but was too tactful to say so. Her hostess adored Russia in quite a fanatical way.

Kira found the Edinburgh children to be delightful. Although endowed with dignified christian names, they were all called by absurd nicknames, like Missy and Ducky, in the privacy of home. Their father was a somewhat remote figure because he was so often away at sea, but now he was still on leave and paid them a lot of attention, especially the six-year-old son, Prince Alfred.

When the Duke of Edinburgh took the prince to London in order to see Greenwich Observatory, Kira was very envious and wished she were able to ask to accompany them, but an ex-Maid of Honour, a guest through kindness of the late Tsarina's daughter, could not be so presumptuous. Alexis had been to Greenwich — worked there, she thought, and all she could do now was ask the little prince questions, explaining she had seen the great Russian observatory. Fortunately Prince Alfred had an inquiring mind so was able to give her descriptions of some of the instruments.

"But fancy you being interested, Mademoiselle. Of course Missy and Ducky are so young, but Mama does not want to hear. She says astronomy is not a subject for females."

Marie of Edinburgh would have been more popular with her English in-laws, had she not displayed an absurd pride in being born a daughter of the Tsar and always fussing about the precedence she considered should be accorded to her. One July afternoon she summoned Kira to write a letter at her dictation to Queen Victoria complaining about some minor infringements of this precedence by one of the latter's daughters. Kira had not reached the end when the Duke of Edinburgh walked into the room and handed his wife a Romanoff-crested letter that had just arrived.

"This looks important, my dear, so I have brought it to you myself. Shall I open it?"

"Do, Affie, but what do you think Papa is writing about? I hope he intends to do nothing rash about the Dolgoruky female."

Not being ordered to retire, Kira remained at the writing table. She heard the Duchess's gasp of horror.

"Affie! Papa has actually married that woman!"

"You mean the female he kept on an upper floor of the Winter Palace? Oh, I say, what bad form! And your mother not dead many weeks ago!"

"Papa says the marriage was formalised the day after St. Peter's fast ended.

236

He had waited fourteen years to marry Princess Catherine Dolgoruky, so did not intend to delay longer. The ceremony took place secretly before four witnesses in a back room at the Elizabeth Palace."

This palace was at Tsarskoe Selo.

"Does your father say if they intend to remain there for a time?"

"They are setting out for Livadia and he will make a public announcement later. However, he declares he has already obtained a Senate decree that she is henceforth to bear the surname Yurievsky, also her children, and that she and they are to be addressed as Serene Highnesses. Oh, Affie, what would dearest Mama think! I ought not to condemn any action by my father the Tsar, God's Anointed, but . . . oh . . . it is too much!"

"Sasha and Minnie will be infuriated."

"They are in Denmark with Minnie's family," said Marie, as if that were some consolation. "At least Papa is not giving that woman the title of Tsarina. She is neither Imperial Majesty nor Imperial Highness. Serene Highness indeed!"

"A temporary measure! You must

prepare yourself for her to be made Tsarina sooner or later."

"Never!" and the Grand Duchess Marie choked back tears of anger.

Naturally no confidences were made to Kira, and as the children were kept in ignorance of the marriage she had not to listen to their innocent remarks about 'Grandpapa Emperor'. That there were shocked discussions among the British Royal family she was well aware. The Prince and Princess of Wales came on a visit to Eastwell, while long letters were written to Queen Victoria. Then life went on as before, Kira secretly worried about her future and lamenting her hasty rejection of Prince Alexis whom she now acknowledged she loved however despicably he had behaved in the past. With faith shaken in Sergei she could not accept his accusations without question as she did once. If only Papa were alive to sort out matters for her!

Lydia wrote twice — the kind of cold, unaffectionate letters Kira knew she could expect. They expressed envy at her sister-in-law's enjoying life amid the British royal circle. How mistaken she is, thought Kira. Lydia herself was very bored with Barona but pleased to be pregnant after eleven barren years of marriage, and impatient for the months to pass when this heir to the Chirnov title and estates would be born and she able to take her place in the Anitchkov Palace set again. Motherhood as such obviously meant little to her. From duty Kira congratulated her and Sergei, secretly thankful for the Grand Duchess Marie's patronage that kept her in England, hoping it would continue for a long time. She did not explain that she was, as she had expected, nothing but an unpaid companion whose services were retained because she was useful. Not that Marie of Edinburgh was an unkind person, but quite incapable of grasping how lonely Kira felt, and easing her conscience, especially over the Tsar's second marriage, by having with her the Maid of Honour so liked by her dead mother. In fact, it was a difficult position to accept the wrong done by a father who was always right and defend him when she mourned for the insult to a beloved mother.

The second item of news imparted by Lydia was the betrothal of Hippolyte to the well-born wealthy widow, Countess Bukaty, and naturally followed by the catty remark that Kira had lost her chance there. "If you do not hurry up you will be an old maid. Sergei and I have done our best for you, and Sergei feels a certain responsibility until you come of age. It is not a responsibility he desires, and frankly we are glad Her Imperial Highness the Grand Duchess has taken a fancy to you. We both hope you will take advantage of her favour and remain in England under her auspices. If she finds you a marriage partner, be less choosy than you were over my attempts."

She was not wanted at Barona, nor when Sergei and his wife were able to return to Petersburg. Kira did not really mind this, but that state of things increased her feeling of loneliness and unwantedness. It was pleasant to remain at Eastwell Park. Here she was adored by the dear little Edinburgh children and useful to their mother. The last-named was in no hurry to hasten back to

London for the season. She preferred to remain in splendid isolation on the Kent estate. Her husband was away at sea.

The Duke of Edinburgh returned near the end of October, and again Kira remained in attendance on Marie while he talked about a visit to the Black Sea when his ship called at the seaport of Varna. He travelled inland to 'Sandro'. Kira gathered that Crown Prince Alexander of Hesse was related to 'Affie'.

"I hope he follows Papa's advice."

"He does, through the sensible representative your father has sent as personal adviser. This is like a red rag to a bull to Sasha."

Sasha was the family abbreviation for Alexander the Tsarevich. Marie was in no danger of confusing the ruler of Bulgaria, 'Sandro', with him. She was annoyed with her brother and his wife because of condemnatory remarks about the Tsar which reached her through the Tsarevna's confidences made to the Princess of Wales, and innocently repeated. Alexandra of Wales did not deliberately make mischief. It was deafness that caused her to be indiscreet.

Then a special letter arrived bearing the Romanoff crest; and Kira, thinking herself summoned to write from dictation an acknowledgment, was given outstanding news by the Grand Duchess Marie.

"His Imperial Majesty is arranging a family gathering in order to introduce his new wife. He has made an — er — morganatic marriage with a certain Princess Dolgoruky. So I shall be going to Petersburg in a fortnight, and you are to accompany me. Not, of course, to attend the family affair, but to become Maid of Honour to this lady, formerly Princess Dolgoruky and now to be called Her Serene Highness, Princess Yurievsky. I was not aware you were previously acquainted with her."

"I happened to save the lady's life from a Nihilist bomb." Kira briefly recounted the incident, then the acquaintance with Prince Alexis, her father's interest in astronomy and the visit to Pulkova.

"I do not recollect you mentioning a previous visit to the Observatory when I and His Royal Highness, the Duke of Edinburgh, took you there."

"Possibly I did not, Ma'am, and I

apologise for the omission, but the memory of my father's death was very painful."

"Had you also met that young astronomer, Prince Alexis Dolgoruky?"

"Yes, Ma'am. My father used to invite him to the house to discuss astronomy with him."

"He is brother to the Tsar's morganatic wife."

"So I gather, Ma'am."

"And for some extraordinary reason is now chief adviser in Bulgaria to the Crown Prince who rules — by courtesy of the Tsar."

"Indeed, Ma'am."

Then the subject was dropped, but Kira was in a state of joy to know she was to become Maid of Honour to the Tsar's new wife. The monarch must have ordered it, and she felt Princess Catherine Yurievsky could not be more formal than the Grand Duchess Marie. She had been pleasant, if cold, that day Alexis took Kira to the private third-floor suite to be thanked for her prompt action in the Summer Garden. And though Alexis was apparently still in Bulgaria, there would be news of him. She might even hope for a meeting one day, but was not likely to have contact with Sergei and Lydia. As devotees of the Tsarevich and Tsarevna, they would ignore the Tsar's second wife as far as they dare.

Regarding the 'Family gathering', Kira was present when the Princess of Wales called on her sister-in-law to impart the contents of a letter just received by her and written by the Tsarevna, the sister 'Minnie'. Marie had gone to London, to Clarence House, for a few days' preparation in purchasing new garments for the Russian trip. Alexandra quickly rushed over from Marlborough House.

"Minnie says that she and Sasha have just returned to Petersburg from the Crimea, where they were obliged to meet that Dolgoruky creature. The Tsar ordered Sasha to summon all members of your Imperial family to assemble at Kolpino Station — not far from Petersburg, and respects are to be paid there. There can be no question of precedence on a railway station, as in a hall of the Winter Palace. That is the reason why. Of course Sasha and Minnie were forced to pay their respects immediately, and Minnie was as glacial as she possibly could be."

"Is Papa intending to create her Tsarina?"

"He said not until a full year after the Tsarina Marie's death."

"Quite right of Papa."

"You always defend him, Marie, but it is completely wrong that he should have married within a month of your mother's death, and created the woman Princess Yurievsky and insisted on her being addressed as Serene Highness."

"What my imperial father does is right in my eyes. He is the Tsar, and I shall behave in accordance with his wishes."

In the middle of November, with real ice outside the station of Kolpino, and an icy atmosphere within, the Imperial train arrived from the Crimea. On the carpet-covered platform decorated with hothouse-grown trees and flowering plants, stood members of the Russian Imperial family. They obediently paid their respects to Tsar Alexander's second wife, then the train continued its journey

245

to the Nicholas Station in Petersburg. Once there, the Imperial couple drove to their private apartments at the Winter Palace.

Wisely the Tsar had avoided such complications as a reception in a drawing-room would entail. There was no question of the youngest female member of the Imperial family taking precedence of Her Serene Highness, as would be the case until she was proclaimed Imperial. Alexander had every intention of granting her that distinction before he created her Tsarina, but he realised he must wait a little. For once he showed tact. The family were ordered to wait in the newly rebuilt banqueting-hall for their host and hostess. At the meal courtesy was observed, but obviously from compulsion and kept to a minimum.

Meanwhile Kira waited in her former Maid of Honour bedchamber, not daring to retire in case the new mistress sent for her. Very weary, she fell asleep in a chair, only being wakened by the maid Anna at midnight. Anna was always correct.

"Her Serene Highness the Princess Yurievsky wishes you to attend her."

10

ONLY once before had Kira actually met the Princess, and that was on the occasion when Alexis took her to the mysterious private suite on the third floor of the Winter Palace. The then Princess Dolgoruky wished to give personal thanks for Kira's prompt action in the Summer Garden which defeated an attempted Nihilist killing.

Now the venue was another one. From secluded third-floor apartments, the Tsar's second wife had moved into rooms formerly occupied by his first partner, and in their previous state familiar to Kira, but decoration and furnishings were different. The late Tsarina had tended to follow her husband in his taste for austerity, but there was nothing austere about her successor's luxurious surroundings.

Kira curtsied respectfully.

The rather cold voice of Princess

Yurievsky said, "Welcome, Kira Vassilievna. At present you are to be my only Maid of Honour and here is your badge."

Kira rose and came forward to receive the badge. She had been given one by the late Tsarina, as was customary, but then there had been warmth shown by the giver. Now there was formality with badge seemingly emphasising difference in rank. Kira saw she need not hope for the affection shown her by Tsarina Marie, nor even by the proud Grand Duchess Marie.

A cold voice continued.

"It was the wish of His Imperial Majesty that the choice of Maid of Honour should fall upon you. He remembers the valuable service rendered by your father in Alaska and Salonika, also the way you saved my life a year ago. Then you are not without experience in the position's duties."

This allusion to her former position with the late Tsarina was most embarrassing, and Kira could only take refuge in making another curtsey and say she trusted she should give satisfaction to Her Serene

Highness. Privately she thought the lady was more beautiful than ever, yet still more withdrawn. Love for the Tsar dominated Princess Yurievsky's life as strongly as when she was Princess Catherine Dolgoruky; and, as Kira was to discover, she continued to preserve that 'apartness', keeping a distance from all except the Tsar and her children. Later, Kira realised that to take an active part in Society would have invited increased censure, and until she actually became Tsarina and was crowned as such it was tactful to remain in the background.

Kira's chief thought now was Prince Alexis, the supposed brother and the only member of the Dolgoruky family who had been kind to the woman who, it was considered, disgraced the proud name by being such a notorious imperial mistress? Was Alexis in Bulgaria, or had he returned to Russia, dividing his time between Petersburg and Pulkova? Etiquette made it impossible for Kira to enquire, but how she longed to know if there were the slightest chance of encountering him. Did the Princess know about the refusal of his offer of marriage?

Most likely she did because Kira felt the Tsar knew — well, something of the matter, and was vexed with her, possibly, for having attracted Alexis in the first place, and for not accepting his attentions. Although Alexis was his son, he could not know Kira behaved as she did because of Sergei's revelations.

She remembered her brother saying the Tsar was known to take a special interest in that particular Dolgoruky, and because of His Majesty's personal intervention he was allowed to leave the Preobrajenski quietly and attend a university abroad. At the Smolny Nobility School, the Tsar had always favoured Kira. Then he made a point of thanking her for saving Princess Dolgoruky's life . . . Oh, that reception at the Anitchkov Palace, and how he ordered her to dance the polonaise with Alexis! Now, although Alexander II was continually coming into his new wife's boudoir, or playing with the children in their nursery, he hardly noticed the Maid of Honour.

His very appearance with a certain physical likeness, whipped up Kira's thoughts about Prince Alexis and her regret at the estrangement between herself and the man she could not deny she loved in spite of Sergei's accusations. Not that Kira blamed her brother. Sergei was not the hero she had always believed him, and he had been spiteful in his condemnation of Alexis, so she clung to the notion that a mistake had been made. A mysterious 'somebody' had falsified, or exaggerated, the cheating at cards that was the cause of Lydia's brother challenging Prince Alexis. It was not exactly a comforting explanation because it still kept Kira in a state of regret that she had not allowed Alexis to tell her his version of the affair.

Olga, the older of the little girls, was celebrating her name-day, this in Russia being considered of more importance than the actual day of birth. Among her presents was a large parcel delivered from the finest shop in Petersburg, and she ran into Princess Yurievsky's boudoir with it, followed by Gogo. Kira was reading aloud from a book that she secretly found boring but knew it had been recommended by the Tsar, who apparently enjoyed it. Therefore the Princess was determined to please him by showing appreciation. Kira remembered at that first interview her surprise when astronomy was discussed with Prince Alexis simply because the Tsar was interested in his son's work at Pulkova.

But Alexis was still in Bulgaria. Kira learnt this now from the excited children.

"Mama, this must be the present Uncle Alexis wrote to say he ordered for me in Petersburg because there was nothing he could buy in that stupid Bulgaria. They don't have shops there."

"They must have some shops, darling, only not the kind we find in Russia."

"It must be an uncivilised place," remarked Gogo who liked to use grand words. "Oh, thank you, Kira Vassilievna."

For Kira had put down the book and begun to assist in opening the very large parcel, then remove layers of inner wrappings.

He went on chattily, "There cannot be proper shops because all the buildings leak. Look how Uncle Alexis said in his last letter to Papa that he had a wooden structure over his bed to keep out the rain, and he stays in the Crown

Prince's palace, but funnily enough it is called a 'konak'. Uncle Alexis says the Turkish sub-ruler, who represented the Sultan, used to live there."

Gogo's exposition was interrupted by Olga pulling away the last of the wrappings and lifting up a huge doll dressed in an elaborate white evening gown, with a long train and a crown on golden hair.

"She is a bride."

"No, she isn't. She is a Court lady. Mama, shall I wear a gown like that when I am grown-up? Will you, too, when the time of mourning for the Tsarina is over and you sit on a throne next to Papa?"

"I expect so."

"But of course you will," declared Gogo. He passed his hand over the doll's hair, saying it was real, not pretend like the eyes that were made of glass. "And the face isn't proper skin but wax."

"How could the eyes and skin be anything else?" came the Tsar's voice.

He had just come into the boudoir, and the children rushed to be hugged by him. Then Olga held up her new doll, explaining it had been sent from

Petersburg, not Bulgaria, because Uncle Alexis could not buy anything like that in Bulgaria.

Of course His Majesty knows all about that country, thought Kira.

She knew Alexis must send regular private reports, just as Papa used to do from Russian America and from Salonika, but the Tsar made no observation about his envoy, only remarked — seemingly to Princess Yurievsky to whom it could be nothing new — that Prince Alexander of Battenberg would ultimately prove an excellent ruler for this backward country newly escaped from the Turkish yoke.

"He has been a distinguished military man but is unversed in politics and diplomacy." Then he directly addressed Kira, "Did your late father say anything to you about Bulgaria after we appointed him to accompany the Crown Prince there?"

Kira said no, adding though that her father had said she must remain in Petersburg while he was absent.

"The Bulgarians are a difficult people. They have been struggling against Turkish oppression for five hundred years, and would never have thrown off the yoke but for Russia. Yet other countries, especially Austria-Hungary, are endeavouring to gain power there."

Strict court etiquette made it impossible for Kira to do more than listen respectfully, however much she longed to ask questions about the role Alexis was playing. She was hoping His Majesty might mention the name of the man she loved, and was inwardly angry that more parcels for Olga should be handed in and everyone's attention directed to them. At last all were opened, examined, and a couple of nurses came to take the children to the nursery for their dinner which was served at midday, earlier than their parents took theirs.

The Tsar had been so distant with Kira during her two periods at Court that she was surprised he should talk directly to her about the backward state of the Bulgarian capital, with its one-storeyed wooden houses, unpaved streets, and utter lack of sanitation. The only grand buildings were the mosques, now little used since liberation.

"The Turks would not permit any

christian church to be as high as a mosque. Was it like that in Salonika, Kira Vassilievna?"

"I do not know, Your Majesty," confessed Kira.

"But you lived there a few years."

Count Chirnov had been the Russian Consul and he did also act as a secret agent, but Kira had no knowledge of that. She explained to the Tsar that her life in Salonika was very restricted by comparison with the years in Russian America because of Mohammedan tradition that kept women secluded.

"I had a governess and spent nearly all my time with her. I do not think there was any social life. In any case, my mother was in bad health. In the end Papa resigned to take her to Switzerland and I came to Petersburg to be a pupil at at the Smolny Nobility School."

"Yes, we remember you there."

For no apparent reason, the Tsar changed the subject of the conversation. He said, "We understand you are much attached to your brother, the new Count Chirnov."

Mention of Sergei brought back the

thought of Alexis, and instinctively Kira knew the Tsar could reveal something concerning the card-cheating and duel which had been missing in Sergei's account. If only she had given Alexis the hearing he wanted! Of course she dare not presume to question His Majesty, but in an endeavour to lead maybe to past events she could refer to the Preobrajenski regiment.

"My brother has resigned from the Preobrajenski and given up all ambition for a military career since becoming Count Chirnov. He is interested in the family country estate."

Interested! Yes, how? Kira thought with shame of Sergei's attitude to the peasants, treating them as if they were still serfs. Aloud she added that he and her sister-in-law were still at Barona.

"You are mistaken, Kira Vassilievna. We saw both of them yesterday when we were walking in the garden of the Anitchkov Palace."

This had become a daily habit of the Tsar in order to take exercise since danger from Nihilist assassination prevented him from using his favourite

Summer Garden. The grounds around the Tsarevich's residence had very high walls and were easy to guard.

"I did not know that," faltered Kira. "I expect Sergei will soon notify me." She was surprised, for the mourning period had not ended. He must have opened his Petersburg house, or had he and Lydia gone to the one previously her home while Papa was alive?

Indicating Princess Yurievsky, the Tsar said, "Her Most Serene Highness will grant you leave to visit them."

Thus Kira found herself allotted a few hours every Tuesday. She was provided with troika and driver, and attended by her maid Anna, but though she was part of the Winter Palace household no guards were considered necessary in this case. Only the Tsar, his wife and children, and members of the Imperial family moved outside with armed protection, and were now forced to occupy palaces that were like beleagured fortresses. The excuse of a year's mourning for the late Tsarina Marie was used to prohibit Court functions, so on the Epiphany feast of 1881 there had been no reception at the Anitchkov as in 1880. Kira guessed Princess Yurievsky was relieved to be spared the ordeal of criticism and unpleasant whispers which would circulate if she appeared in public, and the Anitchkov especially would be an enemy camp.

During the first Tuesday outing, once initial greetings were over, Kira heard censorious remarks from Lydia and Sergei. In vain she said the Princess was at present her mistress and she owed her loyalty.

"Are you betting on this second wife becoming Tsarina and properly crowned? It won't happen if the Tsar dies, you know."

Kira was too shocked by his sneering attitude to make any reply. He was still handsome, but had put on a great deal of weight, and this grossness made him look quite different from the brother she used to worship. She tried now to regard him with affection, but it was not easy, while she despised the way he and Lydia boasted of the favouritism shown to them by the Tsarevich and Tsarevna.

Irritating too was Sergei's harping on being her guardian for another year.

"Although I cannot enforce my wishes, like a suitable marriage, upon you while you remain under the Tsar's wing.

"There is no reason why we should concern ourselves with Kira's matrimonial prospects after her behaviour towards Hippolyte. You have lost him. His betrothal is official now."

"I am very glad," retorted Kira.

Changing the subject she congratulated Lydia on the coming baby. Lydia did not seem particularly thrilled. She remarked that an heir was needed, and Sergei did not expect more than one boy.

"Papa would have been pleased," said Kira, disappointed that her sister-in-law was so unenthusiastic about motherhood.

However, there was a big pretence of happy anticipation when, a minute later, the Tsarevna came to call. She was a charming woman, yet disliked by Kira because of the disloyalty to the Tsar shown by the Tsarevich and wife. The latter had done her duty to Russia. Three sons and a daughter had already proved that, and now she talked wittily about hopes of eventually increasing the number.

"Motherhood is a wonderful experience," said Lydia, and Kira wanted to scream 'Hypocrite!' knowing this remark was only made to impress the Tsarevna.

"Are your duties to His Imperial Majesty's new wife very exacting?" Kira was asked.

"She has come here this morning," interposed Sergei.

Kira was about to say permission had been given her to make regular weekly visits, though inwardly she was beginning to have a doubt that even Sergei, and certainly Lydia, would want to see her so often. She had always known they toadied to the Tsarevich and wife, but never seen it so marked, nor the success they had achieved. The Tsarevna sat there, perfectly at home, and behaving as if no gulf of rank separated them. In a contemptuous tone the imperial lady asked Kira if the latest news from Bulgaria had disturbed Her Serene Highness.

"I don't quite understand what you mean, Madam."

"Oh, the Princess Yurievsky probably

has not heard about her so-called brother's latest exploit yet. The Tsarevich gets news soon after it reaches the Tsar, and he had this only just before I was about to leave the Anitchkov Palace."

"Are you referring to that abominable Prince Alexis Dolgoruky who tried to kill my dear brother by fighting a duel with him?"

"I understand the late Prince Ivan Granovski challenged Prince Alexis," intervened Kira, then saw the look of anger on Sergei's face. "What was the Prince's exploit?"

"Of course, you are somewhat drawn towards that astronomer favourite of His Majesty," drawled the Tsarevna. "You danced very happily at my reception a year ago. Well, I assure you, he has been quite a hero now. There was some plot to poison the Crown Prince Alexander with a headache powder, but Alexis Dolgoruky detected the unusual smell and stopped His Highness of Battenberg from taking it. Won't the Tsar be pleased with the sharpness of that so-called brother of our Tsarina-to-be!"

Lydia and Sergei laughed at their

visitor's wit, but Kira shivered. Supposing Prince Alexis had swallowed the poisoned powder!

"Sandro of Battenberg should never have been chosen by the Tsar as ruler of Bulgaria. Prince Waldemar of Denmark, my own dear brother, would have been a more sensible, and a far more capable ruler."

"We all know that," said Lydia.

Kira knew Sergei was glaring at her, although she carefully refrained from turning her face towards his. He would never cease to dislike Prince Alexis, and whether or not he had given her the correct account of the card-cheating and duel, she felt it was hopeless to question him further on the subject. If there was anything to find out she must discover it from another source. But what source? She was convinced the Tsar or the Princess Yurievsky knew the circumstances of Alexis leaving the Preobrajenski regiment, but a mere Maid of Honour could not presume to question either of those exalted beings. Certainly not the Tsar!

"Surely you should be returning to the Winter Palace, Kira," remarked Lydia, obviously longing to be rid of her sister-in-law.

Kira had another two hours of leave, but there was a shopping errand for Princess Yurievsky she could carry out on the way back, so taking advantage of Lydia's suggestion to make her excuses to the Tsarevna, Kira rose and took leave. Sergei followed her out of the room. She knew what that portended.

They walked down the staircase, but on reaching the hall he drew her into the nearest room.

"You are still hankering after that Alexis Dolgoruky," said Sergei accusingly.

"I refused an offer of marriage made by that gentleman before Papa's death."

"Haven't you been in communication with him since? You and he write to each other . . ."

"I don't know what put that idea into your head. I have not written any letters to Bulgaria. Your description of his character was so unfavourable . . ."

"And very true! Can you swear you have had nothing to do with the

264

scoundrel since I told you what he was really like?"

"He spoke to Papa about proposing marriage to me and though I refused, Papa insisted I saw him, which I did and repeated my refusal. We met once again before his departure to Bulgaria, and that I could not help because I was with the Duke and Duchess of Edinburgh. Now I wonder if I were not too . . . too snubbing."

"Too snubbing, after such presumption!"

"It was not presumption on his part. I had encouraged him."

"I know you did, you little fool!"

Kira tried to sound cool and dispassionate as she asked her brother to explain again what proof he had of Alexis cheating at cards.

"Proof! Do you doubt me, your own brother."

"You could have been mistaken."

"Of course I was not."

Sergei, Kira noticed, had gone an alarming shade of red.

She said, "You told me that Prince Alexis won money from Prince Ivan Granovski because he cheated through

265

using marked cards. A duel followed, but it was stopped before either hurt the other."

"And doesn't cheating at cards arouse your contempt?"

"I cannot believe Prince Alexis did such a thing. Were the cards from a completely new pack, or had they been used by others beforehand? Someone else might have done the marking, and Prince Alexis not known of that tampering."

"What nonsense!"

"You said the Tsar arranged for Prince Alexis to study instead of continuing in the regiment. Well, he must have known that the Prince had done nothing badly wrong. He has shown fondness to him."

Sergei laughed.

"The fondness of a father for his son, however disgraceful the offspring! Yes indeed, he has shown Alexis favour that he never did to the other Dolgoruky wards, excepting of course the Princess Catherine who became his mistress."

"As the rest of the family, excepting Alexis, have been so unpleasant to her, the Tsar would naturally be displeased with them."

"That is how Alexis showed his cunning."

"But the Tsar must believe Alexis, who, you say, is really his son, to be innocent of the card-cheating charge. When a person even a son angers the Tsar, His Majesty shows it. Look at the strained relations between him and the Tsarevich."

Sergei looked murderous at any comparison between the last-named and the man he scornfully referred to as 'Bastard brat of a governess from Hesse.' Ignoring this, Kira asked to be told 'In absolute detail' what happened in the card room, reminding her brother that he had told her he was present while play between the two princes was in progress. As she said this, she suddenly recalled how Sergei had also declared he saw Alexis mark three cards with a pin taken from his cravat, yet it did not make sense for Sergei to know of the fraud before Alexis won from Prince Ivan.

Reminding her brother of this she asked why he did not denounce Alexis at once. Turning redder than ever, he declared she had misunderstood him.

"I can remember your exact words. There is something you have kept from me."

"Nonsense!"

By now thoroughly suspicious, Kira also asked why the story had to be kept from their father.

"I did not want him to know I had been gambling."

"What could it matter years afterwards? Because of the promise you exacted from me, Papa could not understand my refusal to listen to Prince Alexis's proposal of marriage."

"And you wish you had accepted it now," thundered Sergei. "Well, don't dare to encourage the bounder if he offers again on his return from Bulgaria. Legally I am your guardian until you are twenty-one, and whatever the Tsar says I shall refuse to give my consent to your marriage with Prince Alexis Dolgoruky."

How Kira wished it were possible that Alexis would soon come back to Russia and then offer for her, but she knew that to be a vain dream. She had killed his love. He had shown, that last time at Pulkova, how he scorned her. Then how unkind he was when they met at the Winter Palace after the Tsarina Marie's death. She had forgotten to mention that to Sergei but she had been under no compulsion to do so. Guardian indeed! And a whole year must elapse before she reached the age of freedom. Anyway, whatever the Tsar commanded, no subject dare disobey, and she reminded her brother of this.

"Surely you do not want to find yourself in the Peter and Paul fortress as a prisoner, if the Tsar approved my marriage."

"The Tsarevich would see nothing like that happened to me. He is the rising star. Look how the Tsar has aged under constant threat of assassination, for the Nihilists have vowed to kill him as Enemy No. 1."

"They would kill any member of the Imperial family."

"The Tsar is first on the list. In spite of all General Trepov's precautions, neither he nor his subordinates know what hidden would-be killers have slipped through the net. I am thinking of servants in the Winter Palace."

"It would be too risky."

"That means nothing to dedicated Nihilists. They, and I have heard there are women among them, are ready to languish in a dungeon, then go to the gallows, or join the regular procession of prisoners being herded to Siberia."

"Any member of the Imperial family is a target," declared Kira.

"But first and foremost is the Tsar, and he may die any day."

"When the Tsarevich succeeds to the throne, he will be equally vulnerable."

"He will take effective repressive measures. He has always considered his father too lenient. Liberal ideas only give revolutions the chance to explode. Tsar Alexander III will guard against that."

All the same he may get killed, Kira was thinking. She had abandoned any attempt to obtain a more exact account of Prince Alexis's card-cheating, although she was now confident he was guiltless of the offence.

"You had better go back to the Winter Palace and that woman whose Maid of Honour you are. And don't inflict further visits on Lydia and me. You are not a person the Tsarevna wants to meet when she calls here."

Had Sergei really given that cruel, stinging order? Kira sat in the troika, her mind dwelling on the past scene. Sergei had lied to her. It was awful to be disillusioned over a brother you had once respected. Awful to have treated the man you really loved so badly.

Within sight of the Winter Palace, she realised she was arriving back too early. During the coming week she must somehow explain to Princess Yurievsky that the concession giving her regular opportunities to visit Sergei and Lydia was useless because they did not want her, but could she say their Anitchkov Palace engagements kept them too busy to have time for her?

In the meantime she might as well enjoy the rest of today's allotted hours of leisure in doing some shopping. The Princess had ordered a book from England that the Tsar wished to read. If it had arrived a messenger would have brought it, but Kira ignored that possibility, ordered her troika driver to turn round and make for the Nevsky

Prospect as she wished to call at a bookshop in that street.

The owner himself came to pay his respects and make humble apologies regarding the non-arrival of the book in question. He had done his utmost. However, he would immediately write again to London. Kira nodded approval, then told him she would browse around his shelves for a little. It was irritating to have him accompanying her, and she rejoiced to see a familiar figure so had an excuse for getting rid of the owner.

"Good day, Colonel Danilsov."

"Good day, Mademoiselle. Your humble servant," and he would have followed the first bow with a second to take his leave, but Kira detained him.

Dismissing the shop owner, she remarked to Colonel Danilsov that she had been in England since they last met. That had been just after the Tsarina's death.

"Have you been on duty in Petersburg all the time?"

Kira was conscious of bad manners in asking a familiar question of a man she was only meeting for the third time, but he was a close friend of Alexis. Oh, the contrast between Alexis's behaviour towards her during those visits to Pulkova Observatory! Then the last encounter in the Winter Palace when he failed to appreciate her apology, only saying with horrid finality that one could not undo the past.

Possibly not, but one could find out the truth about the past.

Colonel Boris Danilsov had told her he was in the Preobrajenski regiment with Alexis, also that he was the latter's second in the duel fought against Prince Ivan Granovski. She had been about to probe further, but they had to follow the Edinburghs to partake of refreshments offered by Herr Struve. Alexis had joined them and the opportunity was lost.

Not now! Without hesitation the words came out, "Did Prince Alexis really mark playing-cards with a pin he took from his cravat?"

"Who told you that?"

She did not reply immediately that it was Sergei. She was scolding herself for being such a fool that she failed to note the inconsistencies in her brother's accounts the night of the Anitchkov Palace reception. Then Boris repeated the question and she was forced to answer it, blushing at the contempt on Boris Danilsov's face.

"You also knew my brother in the Preobrajenski. I have the impression you did not like him. Is that so?"

"You are correct, Mademoiselle, but of course as his sister your view of him is naturally different."

"It was once, but not now. Sergei has given me different accounts of the card-cheating, and they — well, one must be incorrect, so would you tell me your version of the incident?"

Boris was obviously hesitating. Kira persisted.

"Please forget you belong to the Secret Police, Colonel. What I am asking you about belongs to your days in the Army before transferring to the Third Section, and you are still a friend of Prince Alexis Dolgoruky."

"I ought to have his permission before speaking."

"He offered to tell me the truth, but I believed Sergei and refused to listen to

Alexis's own defence. It was abominable of me. He won't forgive me. Now that I am almost certain Sergei lied . . . Oh, please tell me exactly what happened."

"Your brother was unofficially betrothed to Prince Ivan Granovski's sister, the Princess Lydia, but he had to wait for your father's consent, and Count Chirnov was somewhere in Siberia, travelling back to Petersburg."

"Mama and I were with him. He had been carrying out a diplomatic mission for the Tsar in Russian America. Do go on, Colonel."

"One evening, Alexis, a Count Merpat, and I strolled into a room where Sergei and Prince Ivan had just finished several games, and Sergei said he was playing no more that day or his luck might turn. He had been winning outrageously. Prince Ivan wanted to go on. Sergei disappeared and Alexis good-naturedly took his place. They had finished one game, that Alexis won, when Merpat picked up an ace and said it was marked. Ivan lost his temper, said his future brother-in-law could not have done such a dastardly thing. If he had the Princess Lydia should never marry him. Alexis went to fetch Sergei, and I, knowing his good-nature, was not surprised that Alexis took the blame when the two returned. Ivan challenged him to a duel, and at that time there was an effort to stamp out duelling among officers in the regiment. In spite of this, the two went outside, to fight, Sergei acting as Ivan's second, and I as Alexis's."

"But wasn't the duel stopped?"

"Yes, I think Merpat went straight to the colonel, and all four of us narrowly escaped expulsion from the Preobrajenski. I say the four, but it was only three. The colonel took a serious view of the allegation of Alexis cheating at cards, and being a ward of the Tsar the affair was reported to him. He saw Alexis privately."

"He left, went to a university, and became an astronomer, didn't he?"

"He never wanted to be a military man," said Boris. "And the Tsar being his guardian, — well, he let him have his own way."

More than a guardian, thought Kira.

Aloud she said, "Although Prince

Alexis got his wish, he was branded as a card-cheat, and Sergei should not have let him take the blame."

"Your brother feared disgrace because he wanted to marry Princess Lydia Granovski, and if Prince Ivan had known the truth, then it would have been the end of his hopes."

"But why cheat, and cheat with Lydia's brother?"

"Prince Ivan was a notoriously bad card player, and I think Sergei was in serious financial difficulties. Once your father returned from the east, I believe he confessed his debts to Count Chirnov who paid his creditors."

And Sergei had lied about that, pleading their father must not know about gambling and debts! Kira was aghast. For the first time she was glad dear Papa was dead and had not known Sergei's true character.

11

HOURS of duty as Maid of Honour to the Princess Yurievsky were more clearly defined than had been the case when Kira served the Tsarina Marie, but they involved a great deal of time spent alone, waiting for a summons from Her Serene Highness. No third person was required when the Tsar was present, and he spent most evenings with his beloved, in addition to occasional hours in the afternoon.

Once back in the Winter Palace, Kira went straight to her bedchamber, where Anna was ready to help her change into an evening gown. It was a relief to relate part, although only part, of today's happenings to the faithful maid. Anna had never held a high opinion of Sergei. However, she had never been so outspoken before.

"He was an obedient little boy, Kira Vassilievna, and your respected parents were proud of him, but it was different when they returned from Russian America. The Countess told me how angry the Count was to find Sergei Vassilievich was badly in debt. Of course they were pleased he wanted to become betrothed to one of the grand Granovskis, but that did not make everything right."

"I have never liked Lydia." Kira could speak with a candour she could not show to anyone else. "I scarcely was acquainted with Prince Ivan. Sergei did not seem any different, except that he was charming to me and I admired him so. It is a blow now to find my big brother was never the hero I stupidly imagined he was."

Anna pursed up her lips. She could see her young mistress was upset by learning the truth about him. Aloud, she blamed his wife, but inwardly she thought what a pity Kira Vassilievna had not listened to the proposals made to her late papa by Prince Alexis Dolgoruky. What a splendid husband he would have been for her!

Meanwhile Kira too was thinking about the Prince, and continued to do after she had dismissed Anna and sat alone to wait for the Princess's summons. Officially, she was on duty. There was too much time to think and to repine.

Despite Alexis's passion for astronomy, he had fallen in love with her. And she had not only rejected his proposal of marriage, but irrevocably damaged his pride by blindly accepting Sergei's version of the duel incident. No wonder Alexis lost faith in a woman who so easily accepted that he was a card-cheat and would not listen to his defence. Yes, he helped Sergei out of a serious scrape and Sergei abused the man he cravenly sheltered behind.

He was determined I should think Alexis a villain. I suppose it was because he and Lydia wanted me to become betrothed to that objectionable Hippolyte.

Kira contrasted her lot with that of the Princess Yurievsky who had sacrificed everything for love and never faltered in allegiance to the man who held her heart. Once Kira was critical of such devotion. Now she envied the woman who gave lavishly and without question. Kira had not been Maid of Honour without being convinced of that, also of the Tsar returning such love.

Bitterly she thought now how Alexis would have loved her like that . . . She choked back rising sobs. She dared not indulge in crying when a summons to attend the Princess might come any minute.

She had already made up her mind. Without breaking the rigid etiquette rule prevailing in imperial presence, that any subject of conversation must be introduced by the imperial person, it would be in order for her to thank Princess Yurievsky for the opportunity to visit Sergei. Then, ignoring etiquette, Kira intended to explain why she could make no more Tuesday visits. She should say that the Count and Countess Chirnov were so deeply engaged with attendance at the Anitchkov Palace, neither had any time for her.

Mention of the Anitchkov would certainly anger the Princess against them. So hoped Kira as she entered the small salon where she knew her mistress would be sitting, wanting to be entertained probably by music until the Tsar appeared.

Although in her early thirties, Catherine had not lost a shred of that remarkable beauty which caused the Tsar to fall in love with her. The radiance of her ash-blonde hair made it seem almost golden. Her complexion retained its clear milky look, while her features were perfect, and her expression was calm in spite of constant worry, for the Tsar's life remained in danger from Nihilists. Kira knew Alexander's favourite minister, General Loris-Melikov, had begged him to transfer the centre of government from the Winter Palace, Petersburg, to a palace at Gatchina, which was sixty miles away, or at least remove to Tsarskoe Selo, but the Tsar refused.

"His Imperial Majesty is too busy to join us tonight so we shall require you at dinner, Kira Vassilievna."

Like her husband, the Princess used the imperial we. Her announcement pleased Kira, who saw there would be ample opportunity to make her speech, but for once Princess Yurievsky was in a chatty mood, talking about her children. Only towards the end of the meal did she become silent. Then the servants withdrew and Kira made her opening remarks.

"I thank your Serene Highness for allowing me the time to call on my brother and sister-in-law, and for providing me with the means of getting to their town house."

"Did you enjoy yourself, Kira Vassilievna?"

"Not exactly," blurted out Kira. "Sergei and Lydia are much favoured by Their Imperial Highnesses, the Tsarevich and the Tsarevna. The Tsarevna called on Lydia while I was there. Afterwards I was plainly told that my presence had been intrusive. I gather they do not wish me to repeat my visits."

"Really! You astonish me greatly."

Kira found herself shaking.

"That was the impression I received, Your Serene Highness."

"I thought there was a strong attachment between you and Count Chirnov, your brother."

"Not now."

"Have you quarrelled?"

Kira nodded, trying to steady her

hands. She was aware the Princess was eyeing her keenly, but was surprised when that soft voice asked if the quarrel had anything to do with Prince Alexis Dolgoruky.

Upon Kira acknowledging it had, the Princess said sternly, "You treated my brother with great unkindness."

"I know I did, Your Serene Highness. I was unkind and unfair."

So overwhelmed was Kira by remorse that she hardly noticed how Princess Yurievsky lifted her usual curtain of reserve. Although the supposed relationship between Catherine and Alexis was untrue, yet those two had grown up as brother and sister. Catherine felt an affection for him akin to that of a brother, and it was strengthened by knowing him to be the Tsar's son.

She informed Kira that the monarch told her about the polonaise dance at the Anitchkov reception, and Alexis made her his confidant after Kira's rejection of his offer of marriage.

"He said you accepted without question your brother's lying story of the card fracas and the duel. How could you ever think Alexis capable of such behaviour? Anyone who knew his generous nature would realise he took the blame for your brother."

"But I did not know Prince Alexis so intimately, and I thought I did Sergei, but I was wrong. It still seems incredible that my brother could permit Prince Alexis to ruin his career by taking blame for those marked cards."

"He hated military life, as he confessed to His Imperial Majesty, who agreed to hush up the affair and permit Prince Alexis to go abroad and study. Both assumed that time would cause his expulsion from the Preobrajenski to be forgotten."

"Sergei meanly dragged it up."

"I assume Count Chirnov was opposed to your marriage."

"Yes, he was — that is, Sergei, not Papa. And after Prince Alexis had acted so nobly! But why?"

"If you mean why the present opposition, I should say the present Count has a guilty conscience."

"I wasn't thinking of the present," said

Kira. "I mean, why did he shelter Sergei at the time?"

"According to His Imperial Majesty, Alexis did not want Sergei's marriage to a Granovski to be imperilled. That was such a splendid matrimonial chance for your brother."

"The disgrace would have been a terrible blow for Papa. He and Mama and I were on our way back to Petersburg after being in Russian America."

"His Imperial Majesty thought very, very highly of the late Count Chirnov, and I suspect the desire to spare him the tragedy of an only son dishonoured induced the Tsar to agree to Alexis's urgings. Poor Alexis! He has paid for his foolish martyrdom in losing your love."

Princess Yurievsky rose from her chair and went into the adjoining sitting-room, with Kira following. As Maid of Honour, she would be expected to entertain Her Serene Highness until dismissed. That would only happen when the Tsar appeared.

Oblivious of etiquette Kira declared she was deeply in love with Prince Alexis, but from an interview before he went to

Bulgaria, she feared she had killed his former love for her.

"It has been known for love to revive," remarked the Princess.

"It will not in this case."

"Whether it does or not, you owe it to Prince Alexis to tell him you no longer believe your brother's lies. Who actually revealed the truth to you?"

Kira did not want to mention Colonel Danilsov and avoided answering the question by telling Princess Yurievsky that the last time she saw Prince Alexis she apologised, and he scorned the apology.

"I did not exonerate him from blame because I did not know the full truth until today. I thought — well, the only excuse I have previously been able to make was some mistake on one side or the other."

"Is that what you told Prince Alexis?"

"I don't think I put it quite like that. I can't remember exactly. I was so confused. But I did say I was sorry I had refused to listen to him when he offered to give me his version. He did that when I refused his offer, and he was very upset — well, I ought to have given him a chance. If only I had not been so blinded by what Sergei said!"

"How did my brother receive your apology?"

"He . . . well, it was some time later, and he had naturally grown bitter. He said something about facts being unalterable and one could not undo the past. How I wish I had known of Sergei's perfidy then, but it was only today. Prince Alexis will never forgive me!" And with this, Kira nearly broke down and sobbed. With a struggle, she wiped her eyes and said, "I beg Your Imperial Highness's pardon."

"I can see you do care for him, Kira Vassilievna."

"I do, but it is useless."

"All the same, when I next write to him, I shall tell him you have discovered his innocence and your brother's guilt."

Such kindliness from the aloof Princess quite threw Kira off her balance. She fell on her knees, then kissed her mistress's skirt.

"Thank you, Your Serene Highness.

I cannot, dare not hope for the return of his love, but it will be a comfort always to know I ... I mean for him to know ... "

"That it was your brother, not mine, who was the villain of the piece," remarked the Princess.

"When is he likely to return from Bulgaria?" Kira ventured to ask.

"I have no idea. His Imperial Majesty will not recall Alexis while the Crown Prince of Bulgaria needs his help. You see my brother is absolutely loyal and trustworthy, and the Tsar has few men of which he can say that. Your father was one, and when he died, His Imperial Majesty asked Prince Alexis to make the sacrifice, that is, to give up his astronomical work at Pulkova for an indefinite period. 'We can rely on you to give true reports,' said His Majesty."

In the adjoining room, Kira was ordered to play the guitar. Evidently the Princess considered she had talked enough. Kira still had not recovered from the unusual condescension and played poorly in consequence. However, the second piece of music was interrupted by the entrance of the Tsar, looking almost boyishly excited.

As Kira left the room after receiving a nod of dismissal, she heard him say, "Loris-Melikov has been showing me the manifesto's initial draft." The contents of any such document were of course unknown to Kira, but she had a shrewd idea this manifesto would embody reforms the Tsar had for some time been anxious to introduce. Although he had taken the drastic step of abolishing serfdom, thus being called the Tsar Liberator, yet it was long known he was not content with that and wished to do more in spite of horrified government reactionaries, especially his Heir.

Even household gossip at the Winter Palace revealed to Kira how the Tsarevich hated the Tsar's favourite minister. General Loris-Melikov held liberal views, but danger from the Nihilists made him urge the monarch to withhold any constitutional reform until these men of subversive action had been crushed. Apparently they had now, thought Kira, if some important manifesto was to be issued, for the Tsar would not be exuberant if it contained repressive measures.

His manner towards Kira changed completely after this evening, so she guessed Princess Yurievsky must have confided in him about Alexis and herself. Instead of being coldly formal, he smiled upon her as he used to when she was a pupil at the Smolny, was not insistent on her leaving the room every time he appeared but ordered her to remain, and he even talked about state matters to his wife in front of Kira.

She sometimes thought he spoke of Bulgaria deliberately because he was aware of her interest. Of course there was nothing secret in his statements, which concerned matters of general knowledge about the terrain of the country and its long struggle to gain independence, thus ending the people's sufferings under the Turk. For the Bulgarians were Christians and did not take kindly to Moslem overlords.

It was Russian military might that finally freed the country from the Ottoman Empire, and, once free, the Bulgarians asked Tsar Alexander II to choose a ruler. He had to be a foreign prince since there was no native royalty, nor a suitable commoner to occupy the vacant position. Actually the Tsar's choice was not very suitable for Prince Alexander of Battenburg's brilliant military career had done nothing to fit him for political life. Submissive to his uncle, the Tsar of Russia, he floundered in attempts to put down rebels and intriguers, from outside as well as within.

To help 'Sandro', Alexander II had decided to make the late Count Chirnov personal adviser to the Crown Prince, and go-between, but with the Count's death in the Winter Palace bomb explosion, the Tsar was at a loss. Although he disliked taking Prince Alexis from astronomical work at Pulkova, he felt this bastard son was the only Russian he could trust for plain, unexaggerated reports on what was happening in Bulgaria, although he had none of the experience to advise Crown Prince Alexander that the late Count Chirnov would have had.

"You are sensible," Alexis was told.

"You must check Sandro if he wants to act rashly. He understands he must confide in you and that you will keep me informed about all that happens. Be tactful and cautious. That I do urge you."

"I am an astronomer," said Alexis, nearly adding that he was not an astrologer, but thought his father might not appreciate the joke. "I will do my utmost, sire, to carry out your commands."

"You will serve my purpose, in spite of your lack of experience."

The Tsarevich would not have agreed with that, for he was furious about any favour being shown to a man who was his illegitimate half-brother.

He said so to the Tsarevna, referring to Prince Alexis being expelled from the Preobrajenski. She agreed. Her aversion to Germans was strong, so she disliked Crown Prince Alexander and it was a perpetual grievance with her that the Tsar had chosen him for Bulgaria, not her own brother, Prince Waldemar.

The appointment had been made after the Winter Palace explosion, and during the months Alexis had been in Bulgaria he had to send his unacknowledged father regular reports, also descriptions of Bulgaria. At first the Tsar studied them with close attention, but now, in February 1881, the Tsar was paying that country less attention. He intended to send for Prince Alexis to return in person for a short time, and then he hoped to patch up the love affair that had gone wrong. He had been touched by Catherine's account of Kira's misery, and though his position as Tsar would not permit him to mention the matter to a mere Maid of Honour, yet he was anxious for the match. He loved this unacknowledged son and he thought Kira Vassilievna Chirnov would make a fine wife.

Yes, he told himself, I must summon Alexis, telling Sandro that a personal discussion is essential. Then the two lovers shall meet and, I hope, reconcile their differences. Of course, Kira Vassilievna will be under age for a whole year, but that abominable Sergei Vassilievich shall be threatened with Siberia unless he consents to his sister's marriage.

However, any action of this lesser, personal nature was impossible until he had brought out his new manifesto and seen it accepted. The document was nearly completed by General Loris-Melikov. It concerned a radical reformation of the existing Council of State, a feeble body, and ultimately the Tsar hoped the way would be clear to granting full franchise to all Russians. A far-off dream in a vast country, most of whose inhabitants were illiterate, but the Tsar Liberator saw it as the aim he had always had in mind and hoped to achieve during his lifetime. Hadn't he brought about freedom for the serfs, something ministers and advisers declared to be impossible?

At a quarter to one every Sunday, the Tsar left the Winter Palace for the Michael Riding School where he reviewed troops on its parade ground. Once he used to ride on horseback, but now he drove in a closed vehicle with an escort of Cossacks and followed by two others containing police officials. He only changed to horseback on reaching the Riding School.

It was the end of February in Russia,

where the old system of calendar reckoning remained in force, but the date in western countries was the thirteenth of March. In England people were beginning to think of spring. In Russia it was still deep winter.

Seeing the Tsar leave Princess Yurievsky's boudoir with sprightly step and an almost smiling countenance, Kira thought how marked was the likeness to Alexis. Then a strange shivering seized her. She was not a superstitious person but a horrible foreboding came to her that this was the last time she should see Tsar Alexander alive. She must not be so foolish. Danger of assassination was always present, but he had survived many attempts on his life and on this occasion he would be particularly well guarded. She went into her mistress's room.

The Princess was in a sparkling, friendly mood.

"His Imperial Majesty is very happy. Kira, you have heard him speak of the manifesto he instructed General Loris-Melikov to prepare. Much work has gone into it because His Majesty made many alterations, but at last it is perfect and ready for the imperial signature. It will be published tomorrow and all the world will learn what privileges are planned for the Russian people."

Luncheon was taken in company of Gogo, Olga, and little Catherine.

"Don't we wait for Papa's return from the military parade?" asked Gogo.

"No, darling. Papa will not be back until nearly three o'clock. After the parade he told me he should pay a call on his cousin, the Duchess of Mecklenburg. No, you have not met the lady, Gogo. She has only come to Petersburg for a short stay."

"Why does she not come to see Papa? He is the Tsar."

"She will come to the Winter Palace one day," replied Princess Yurievsky.

When you are Tsarina, she and her mother, the Grand Duchess Elena Pavlovna, will be obliged to pay their respects, thought Kira. As it was, any members of the Imperial family who could contrive to avoid Princess Yurievsky did so. Kira was not to know that this particular cousin, the Grand Duchess Catherine, Duchess of Mecklenburg, would be the last relative of Tsar Alexander to see him alive.

After lunch the Princess complained of a headache, and retired to lie down for an hour or so. The children were taken back to their nurseries, and after seeing the dresser change Her Serene Highness's gown for a negligée and that she was comfortable in bed, Kira sat alone, on duty, awaiting a summons. At these frequent times she had developed the habit of drifting off into a day-dream where she was walking through a wood in early summer with Prince Alexis. Today the day-dream eluded her. She was possessed by the conviction that tragedy was impending. She was certain something had happened, or was about to happen, to the Tsar.

Finding it impossible to remain at her post any longer, Kira left the imperial private apartments. Ignoring the guards stationed at top of the main staircase, she walked halfway down it and leant against the marble balustrade, waiting apprehensively. None of the guards moved. They knew her as attendant to the Princess Yurievsky and therefore privileged to walk about the palace unchallenged.

Time had lost all meaning for Kira. She just stood and watched and waited. Suddenly there was commotion at the entrance door which had been opened to admit bloodstained Cossacks carrying a stretcher on which a person — or was it a corpse? — was lying. A man on each side endeavoured to staunch blood flowing from it as the procession moved.

Boris Danilsov, dishevelled and with splashes of blood on his uniform, came darting up the staircase.

"They are taking the Tsar to his private study. Come away. You must not see the terrible sight. But the Princess must be informed."

"The Princess is sleeping," Kira managed to say. "I will go to her, but first tell me what happened. Is the Tsar dead?"

"He lapsed into unconsciousness on the snow before they lifted him up. He was terribly injured by that second bomb. The first missed him."

"Tell me before I break the news to

the Princess," urged Kira.

It seemed the Tsar was on his way to the Winter Palace after leaving his cousin, and because he was late and had promised his wife to be home by three, he urged the coachman to take a short cut by the Catherine Canal Quay. Uniformed police and plain clothes men were planted amongst the crowd on the official route, but not on this quay unexpectedly used by the imperial vehicle.

Later it was discovered that a Nihilist disguised as a herring-girl saw the sleigh turning right instead of left and signalled to an accomplice who rushed after it and threw a bomb in front of the horses. It exploded, killing two Cossacks, but leaving unharmed the Tsar, who stepped out of his sleigh to help the casualties. Immediately another Nihilist threw a second bomb which killed or injured several people, including the Tsar.

Boris Danilsov escaped and went to the monarch, who lay bleeding in the snow. His face and hands were covered with wounds, while one leg had been shattered and the other completely severed by the explosion.

"He was barely conscious then," Boris told Kira. "Doctors are attending him but there is nothing they can do. Now how is the news to be broken to Her Serene Highness?"

Kira never quite remembered how she did this. When the Princess grasped the truth, she shrieked hysterically, then insisted on going down to the study, caring nothing for her undressed state. Kira and Boris followed her.

The Tsar was unconscious and had no knowledge that the woman he loved so passionately was sobbing on his chest, her negligée soaked in blood, nor could he hear her repeated cries of Sasha, his pet name.

Tsarevich, Tsarevna, and other members of the family appeared as if by magic. Kira's intimation of the Tsar's actual passing was when a doctor, who had been feeling the pulse, let the hand fall and approached the Tsarevich.

Immediately everyone in the room, except the hysterical Princess Yurievsky and the Maid of Honour attending her, was doing homage to the new monarch, Tsar Alexander III.

12

DURING the two succeeding days and nights, Kira hardly left Princess Yurievsky, only doing so to see the children and try to comfort them. It was disturbing to find ten-year-old Gogo and his slightly younger sister Olga so overcome with grief, while little Catherine could not believe she should never see 'Papa' again.

On the afternoon of the second day, Kira brought the three to their mother's bedside, hoping the sight of them would induce the Princess to cease from weeping and make her feel the children of that great love needed her. She must struggle through the rest of her allotted span of life although the man she adored was dead.

"I will always look after you, Mamma," said Gogo. "Papa is looking down on us from heaven and he expects it."

As Kira had judged, the children's presence did have a bracing effect. The violence of the Princess's grief subsided.

She passed a quiet night, and when the Court physician visited her the next morning he was very pleased with her. He must have reported this to the new Tsar for, in the afternoon, there was an enquiry if she felt well enough to receive His Majesty who had called.

"I must," said the Princess, dropping the imperial we. "Where is he?"

"In the green drawing-room, Your Serene Highness."

There were a few black gowns in her wardrobe. One was quickly donned and, ordering Kira to attend her, the Princess hurried to this small reception room in the private apartments.

The great giant of a Tsarevich had always hated the woman whom he considered supplanted his mother, but regarded it as his duty to obey any command laid down by his father. Now Tsar Alexander III was the supreme authority and Kira trembled inwardly as to how he might exert that authority.

After acknowledging his stepmother's obeisance and giving her permission to be seated, he declared a letter from "His late Imperial Majesty made arrangements concerning the financial position of you and your children. We shall strictly adhere to those."

I should think so, thought Kira, who had not been dismissed so stood behind Princess Yurievsky's chair.

The date of the funeral was stated. This, of course, could not be at once because for a Tsar there must be a public lying-in and, as foreign royalties or their representatives would be attending, time had to be allowed for them to reach Petersburg. Would Alexis come? Kira knew the Crown Prince of Bulgaria would do so; therefore, considering his close relationship — however secret — with the late Tsar, Alexis must come with him.

Giving her attention to what the new Tsar was saying, she was somewhat shocked to hear him banning Princess Yurievsky from attending the funeral. A dreadful command to give to the widow when all female members of the Imperial family would be there, but Kira understood why. The difficulty of precedence cropped up. On this occasion, Princess Yurievsky must have first place of honour and be at the head of the procession and escorted by Tsar Alexander III, while his wife, the new Tsarina, followed behind. Princess Yurievsky grasped the reason as well as Kira did, but she realised protest was futile, so bowed her head in acquiescence.

Coldly, though not in an unkind tone, Alexander III continued. He looked so bovine, thought Kira. Yet he held the fate of millions in his huge hands.

"We desire you and your children to leave Russia immediately after the funeral. You must never return. Reside abroad where you wish, and the financial sum provided for your needs by His late Imperial Majesty shall be forwarded at regular intervals."

The Princess bowed her head again, then said she wished to be accompanied by her present household, as well as her children. It needed the Tsar's official permission, usually given through the Third Section, for any Russian to go abroad.

"A list of your household is being prepared."

"Then I trust it will include my Maid

of Honour, Kira Vassilievna Chirnov, who has been such a comfort to me. She has an old personal maid, a peasant woman called Anna . . . "

"Kira Vassilievna Chirnov has not yet attained her majority, so permission from her guardian, Count Chirnov, is required."

Kira froze. Sergei might well refuse permission out of sheer malice. Possibly Princess Yurievsky sensed the possibility.

"Count Chirnov cannot disobey a direct command from Your Imperial Majesty. I need Vassilievna. She has been such a comfort to me since . . . "

Here the Princess acted wisely, although she was too overwhelmed with grief to think deliberately of doing so. A sudden vision of the good-looking, intelligent Tsar, very different from the new monarch who sat opposite her, made her burst into tears. This display of grief actually touched Alexander III. Stolid and unimaginative as he was, he worshipped his own wife, so was able to comprehend how this widow was shattered by the loss of his father, much as he had always condemned, and still did, the liaison. 'Minnie' had told him 'Dear Sergei and Lydia' wanted to have 'that young, irresponsible sister' in their home until she came of age, but in spite of that he found himself promising Princess Yurievsky that Kira Vassilievna and her maid should be granted the required permission with passports to prove it.

Although the former Princess Dagmar of Denmark was now the Tsarina Maria Feodorovna and exerted a powerful influence over her husband, she was clever enough never to cross swords openly with him. Her dear friend, Countess Lydia Chirnov — still looking ill after a miscarriage — declared the Count and she desired to resume charge of Kira Vassilievna until the girl became of age.

"We never approved of her becoming Maid of Honour to that Princess Yurievsky. Kira can lapse into most foolish behaviour and Sergei dreads her becoming involved with an unsuitable *parti*."

"Like the pretended Prince Alexis Dolgoruky," said the Tsarina, quick to grasp the drift of her dear friend's meaning. "Oh, those dances at our reception a year ago! You do dislike that astronomer."

"He cheated my dear brother at cards, then fought Ivan in a duel that was fortunately stopped before injury was inflicted." To do Lydia justice she was ignorant of the real facts, believing what Ivan and later Sergei told her. "Yes, I hold Alexis Dolgoruky in utmost contempt and should rejoice to see him publicly disgraced."

She reported this conversation later to Sergei.

He replied, "Kira knows I should never allow her to marry that man. I have no proof there is anything between them, but I suspect she hankers after him, and he is an unscrupulous climber. Astronomer indeed!"

"If he wanted he could meet her abroad while she is with that woman."

"Um! Of course, he is accompanying the Crown Prince of Bulgaria who has been invited to attend the funeral, but he must not be allowed to return to that country. I shall speak to the Tsar. His Majesty has no use for the Battenberg prince. He thought it absurd of the late Tsar to plan sending my father as adviser."

"Was it informer rather than adviser? And when your father died he was replaced by a man who would make secret as well as routine reports to His late Majesty. All very carefully arranged and so easy to accomplish!"

"That is an idea, Lydia. I shall hint about spying to the Tsar, and that will be enough for him to instruct the Third Section to watch Alexis Michailovich Dolgoruky with a view to arrest."

Tsar Alexander III, his wife and children remained in their old home, the Anitchkov Palace, and gave hospitality to foreign royalties arriving for the funeral. Meanwhile the former ruler's body lay in the great malachite hall at the Winter Palace, where once admission was so strict; but now any Russian subject — wealthy or poor, aristocrat or peasant — might file past the open coffin.

Public grief was intense. Had not the Tsar Liberator abolished serfdom? And it was whispered around that he had prepared a manifesto which would introduce an elementary form of representative government. Nihilists prevented that manifesto from being signed, and signed it would never be, for the same liberal ideas were not held by his successor. Alexander III was, and always had been, a reactionary. Nor had he the same caring for his subjects. Unlike Alexander II, he would not have exclaimed after the first bomb, "Thank God, I am untouched! I must see to the wounded." Directing attention to those casualties, the Tsar was fatally injured by a second bomb.

Injuries to his lower limbs were concealed by a rug as he lay in the coffin, while the head was partly hidden by bandages. He had left directions that no medals or decorations were to be placed on his chest for burial, but Princess Yurievsky, to Kira's and others' horror, cut off her long fair locks and placed them on the corpse before the coffin was finally closed.

Forbidden to attend the funeral, she leant on Kira and together they watched from an upper window the procession leave the Winter Palace on its journey to the Cathedral of SS. Peter and Paul on the opposite bank of the River Neva. Almost unnaturally calm, she waited until it was out of sight, then retired to her bedchamber, but managed first to give Kira full instructions regarding packing for her departure abroad.

"We leave Russia at the earliest possible moment."

So Kira issued orders to dresser, nurses, and other servants who would be coming; and as her mistress wished to be alone for the rest of that sad day, she devoted herself to Gogo, Olga, and the little Catherine, trying to entertain them with old Russian folktales. Fantasy was better than reality. In any case she had no idea what was Princess Yurievsky's destination abroad, nor did she greatly care. If only she could meet Alexis before she left Russia! Surely he would have arrived with the Crown Prince of Bulgaria, though, unlike the latter, he could probably be no more than a mere spectator among the crowds lining the processional route. And his so-called sister did not mention his name.

Her heart leapt with a mixture of joy and apprehension when one of her stories was interrupted by somebody entering the room and the children called out his name in chorus.

He was here at last. She recalled their last meeting; that day at Pulkova when the Duke and Duchess of Edinburgh decided to visit the observatory and Alexis had behaved towards her with a coldness that made it only too clear he had thrust her out of his life. Again, in the Winter Palace, she despaired of winning him back. Yet she clung to hope and was still clinging.

She rose to her feet, conscious he was hugging the children, but unable to control her trembling and give a polite greeting.

Had he received that letter the Princess intended to write, saying Kira Vassilievna was no longer duped by Sergei? Would it be possible to tell Alexis she had learnt the true facts from Colonel Boris Danilsov? If the children had not been present . . .

Then she realised the children did not matter, for somehow he knew everything. There was no need to crave forgiveness. Before she could lift her eyes her hot hands were grasped by his cool ones, but the lips pressed on the back of one hand were burning with passion. Could it be Prince Alexis himself who was asking her pardon?

"See the doll you gave me for my name day, Uncle Alexis."

"Wait while I get my bicycle, Uncle Alexis, and show you how I can ride it."

"I got lots of dollies, Uncle Alexis, but I want a big one like Olga has. I getting a big girl."

He was doing his utmost to get rid of the importunate children so that he and Kira could be alone, and she guessed that. To be alone with the man she wanted to marry — yet she would not be free to do that until she was twenty-one for Sergei would never give his consent. Besides, she must go abroad for a short time with the bereaved Princess Yurievsky . . .

Kira awoke next morning radiant with happiness. At last Alexis and she had reached an understanding, and though duty would keep them apart for some months, what did that matter when their ultimate happiness was assured?

She had told Alexis she recognised what the pursuit of astronomy meant to him, but he swore that was no obstacle to married life, provided she did not mind leading a somewhat secluded existence.

"Which you know is the kind of life I like. Society has no lure for me. You will continue at Pulkova, won't you?"

When released from the Bulgarian assignment, that was his intention. He might even try to obtain a post in some observatory abroad, like the world-famous Greenwich, or one of the new ones springing up in the United States. Remembering those happy days in Russian America, Kira thought she would love to make a new home for Alexis in that continent. However, he must continue service to the Crown Prince of Bulgaria, with whom he had become on friendly terms, and was indeed much attached to this Hessian prince, as was Kira to Princess Yurievsky . . .

And today, Alexis would be calling at the Winter Palace to see his bereaved 'sister', and when he did Kira expected to be called from her work of organising

314

packing for the Yurievsky departure. A summons came during the morning, but no Alexis. The Princess told her she had received an order from the Tsar with necessary documents. She and her party were to leave Petersburg and proceed on their journey abroad the day after tomorrow.

"Tsar Alexander III is positively flinging me out of the country," said Catherine indignantly. "And I shall not humble myself to ask for a longer interval. Everything must be ready for us to leave at the time ordered. By the way, your brother, Count Chirnov, brought the Tsar's instructions. I offered to call you, as with so little time left it would be awkward to spare you to visit him for an official farewell. My dear, I am sorry to tell you this, but he declared bluntly that neither he or his wife had any wish to see you, as you had been a most difficult ward. Of course I could see he was angry I had obtained permission to take you abroad with me."

There was too much to be done for further talk. Kira felt awkward about mentioning Alexis's visit yesterday, but the Princess on that tragic day had refused to see anyone; and she must have heard from the children this so-called brother had been ready to see her if she could have borne to receive anybody immediately after the funeral of her beloved. But why did not Alexis come today? Perhaps the Prince of Bulgaria was detaining him, decided Kira, hoping he would appear later.

Evening was well advanced when Anna, who always seemed to know what was happening, whispered to Kira that Prince Alexis Dolgoruky was closeted with Her Serene Highness. Kira, counting the row of trunks assembled in a corridor, continued her task with beating heart, at last being rewarded with a summons from the Princess to the small yellow salon. There she found Alexis, but before he could greet her, Catherine rose, put her arms around Kira, and lovingly called her "my sister-to-be."

"Alexis has told me that you two understand each other at last. I am very happy for you, and so would my dear husband have been if he had lived." She gave a gulping sob, then bravely went on.

316

"Alexis is in a great hurry. He is obliged to go to the Pulkova Observatory tonight, and, alas, he cannot return before our departure."

"I have duties I cannot avoid," said Alexis, and Kira saw his eyes pleading with her to accept this speedy leave taking.

For how long was the separation to continue?

"It just needs patience before the two of you can be united in matrimony, and I hope to see that done without Count Chirnov's consent, Kira, on your coming of age. But Alexis must not delay any longer. Goodbye, dear brother." And the Princess left the room.

"There is something wrong, Alexis. What is it?"

"Only this hateful parting," and he swept Kira into a passionate embrace, pressing his lips to hers again and again, then only ceasing as if by a tremendous exercise of will.

"Must you really go to Pulkova tonight?"

He nodded, pulled her to him just once more, then almost pushed her aside to fling on his sable-lined cloak and fur-trimmed cap that had been lying on a chair. Saying, "Goodbye, my darling," he positively ran from the room.

After a moment's hesitation, Kira followed, but he went along different corridors and so quickly that she lost him. The lighting was dim, evidently an economy until the new Tsar moved there.

Kira pulled back a curtain from a window, hoping to catch a last glimpse of Alexis, and was rewarded by the sight of him emerging from a back entrance. A three-horsed sleigh was drawn up and there was a waiting man beside it. As Alexis got in and the other followed, Kira saw he was Colonel Boris Danilsov.

She mentioned this later when alone with Princess Yurievsky.

"The Colonel is high up in the Third Section, or Secret Police, but he and Alexis are old friends."

"What of it?" The Princess sounded very brusque. "Kira, do not mention Alexis's name, or say anything about your understanding with him — not until we are out of Russia."

"I know something is amiss. Please tell me. He is worried."

"Because the Crown Prince of Bulgaria has been snubbed by the Tsar, who never approved of His Imperial Majesty assisting that country, or his ruler. But that is no business of yours or mine, and there is too much for you to do to waste time in gossip."

"Regarding Alexis . . . "

"Remember, you know nothing about him. Say so if asked."

Although silenced, Kira was vaguely uneasy, but could do nothing, and, as Princess Yurievsky said, there was so much to do and they must be ready to leave in accordance with imperial orders.

With so much work on hand, it was inconvenient to be summoned to the Anitchkov Palace by the Grand Duchess Marie of Edinburgh, who had come to attend her father's funeral and now wished to see Kira Vassilievna Chirnov before leaving Russia.

The interview was pleasant. The Grand Duchess had been kind in the past and was now, and Kira said goodbye with a certain regret when she was dismissed. Then, on leaving the palace, she had the misfortune to meet Lydia. It seemed in order to offer polite apologies for not being able to call on her sister-in-law.

"Sergei told that Yurievsky woman that neither of us wished to see you ever again."

Kira gasped.

"Anyway, you will never marry that astronomer she calls brother. I suppose you know His Imperial Majesty has ended the ridiculous appointment to the Bulgarian prince, so Alexis Dolgoruky will not be going back there."

The Princess had said, 'Remember you know nothing about him. Say so if asked.' But in this case Kira did know what Lydia was talking about, and mercifully Lydia was too busy talking to notice her audience's surprise.

"I have just heard Prince Alexis has returned to the Pulkova Observatory. Not that he will be permitted to remain there long! Sergei has the Tsar's confidence, you see, and we were determined you should have no chance of renewing your former acquaintance with the late

Tsar's bastard. As for that upstart, the Crown Prince of Bulgaria, well, Tsar Alexander III will not listen to his appeals for help. Enough money has been wasted already."

"I know nothing about the subject," Kira managed to say. "When my Papa was going there as envoy, he gave me no information."

"Envoy! Sergei and I guessed he was spying for the late Tsar, as has Alexis Dolgoruky. Yes, he will have to undergo questioning by the Third Section when Alexander of Battenberg has returned to Bulgaria. And there is to be a purge of officials in the Third Section and other government departments. The new Tsar has already sent General Loris-Melikov in banishment to the Caucasus."

The thought came to Kira that Boris Danilsov might be quitting his post. Perhaps he and Alexis were not going to Pulkova. Then she pulled herself together, endeavouring to look at a loss to understand Lydia. She was successful.

"Of course you know nothing of these matters. I don't suppose the late Tsar talked political secrets in front of you."

"He certainly didn't," Kira could reply truthfully.

The two women parted, Lydia saying with final spite, "I have never forgiven Alexis Dolgoruky for cheating my brother at cards, so I, for one, will be delighted to see him imprisoned, then executed for spying. That is what will happen. You mark my words."

With Catherine Yurievsky's warning pounding through her brain, Kira kept absolutely silent and left her sister-in-law without even saying good-bye. Back in the Winter Palace, she went straight to the Princess's boudoir and finding her alone poured out the story.

"Surely Alexis cannot be arrested for spying. Is it possible to warn him?"

"My dear Kira, the Crown Prince of Bulgaria learnt about this charge, and he told Alexis. It had been made by your brother to the Tsar. Alexis has been forbidden to leave Russia and his passport withdrawn."

"Oh, no!"

"Everything is going to work out all right, my dear. Alexis told me the whole plot but did not want to worry you. He

322

is to be arrested as soon as the Crown Prince departs."

"I saw Alexis get into a sleigh last night with Colonel Danilsov . . . "

"Who has defected from his post. He and Alexis are on their way to Odessa."

"Odessa! But that is in the south of Russia."

"A port on the Black Sea where the yacht *Alexander* lies. It belongs to the Crown Prince, and is therefore Bulgarian territory, and it is waiting to take the ruler back to Bulgaria. That ruler, despised by the present Tsar because he is of German birth, can obtain no further assistance regarding Bulgaria, and would have left by now, but is delaying his departure for Alexis and Colonel Danislov to get aboard. Oh, they have false passports. Remember, the Colonel has had access to such documents in Secret Police files."

"You mean, Third Section officials will go to Pulkova to arrest Alexis, but he will be safe on the Bulgarian ship by then?"

In spite of her own tragic bereavement, Princess Yurievsky smiled happily as she reassured Kira all would be well with Alexis. Safe in that Balkan country, they would be married.

"Kira, my dear, you must be very patient and very controlled. We are going straight to Vienna, and as soon as he can Alexis will communicate with us from Bulgaria. Crown Prince Alexander wants me to bring you to his capital, where, ignoring your unpleasant brother, he himself will authorise your marriage in one of the Orthodox churches there, for those churches survived in spite of Turkish oppression."

It seemed an endless journey, then a long wait in Vienna, until word came that Alexis and his friend were safe and on their way up the Danube to meet Princess Yurievsky, her children, and Kira at a Bulgarian town called Rustchuk.

"I cannot endure remaining in the capital until you actually arrive," wrote Alexis.

From Vienna to Budapest, then further along the Danube river, reaching Rustchuk at last, just as Alexis arrived there, ready to escort the party to the capital where the wedding would take place.

"But studying the heavens," said Kira

after the joy of reunion had subsided a little. "You know I never want to come between you and your beloved astronomy."

"Your love and possessing you means more to me than that," he told her. "All I can think of now is to make you my wife, but whatever future lies in store for us, we shall be together. I can live without Pulkova Observatory. I should not want to live without you."

THE END

THE WILDERNESS WALK
Sheila Bishop

Stifling unpleasant memories of a misbegotten romance in Cleave with Lord Francis Aubrey, Lavinia goes on holiday there with her sister. The two women are thrust into a romantic intrigue involving none other than Lord Francis.

THE RELUCTANT GUEST
Rosalind Brett

Ann Calvert went to spend a month on a South African farm with Theo Borland and his sister. They both proved to be different from her first idea of them, and there was Storr Peterson — the most disturbing man she had ever met.

ONE ENCHANTED SUMMER
Anne Tedlock Brooks

A tale of mystery and romance and a girl who found both during one enchanted summer.

CLOUD OVER MALVERTON
Nancy Buckingham

Dulcie soon realises that something is seriously wrong at Malverton, and when violence strikes she is horrified to find herself under suspicion of murder.

AFTER THOUGHTS
Max Bygraves

The Cockney entertainer tells stories of his East End childhood, of his RAF days, and his post-war showbusiness successes and friendships with fellow comedians.

MOONLIGHT
AND MARCH ROSES
D. Y. Cameron

Lynn's search to trace a missing girl takes her to Spain, where she meets Clive Hendon. While untangling the situation, she untangles her emotions and decides on her own future.

NURSE ALICE IN LOVE
Theresa Charles

Accepting the post of nurse to little Fernie Sherrod, Alice Everton could not guess at the romance, suspense and danger which lay ahead at the Sherrod's isolated estate.

POIROT INVESTIGATES
Agatha Christie

Two things bind these eleven stories together — the brilliance and uncanny skill of the diminutive Belgian detective, and the stupidity of his Watson-like partner, Captain Hastings.

LET LOOSE THE TIGERS
Josephine Cox

Queenie promised to find the long-lost son of the frail, elderly murderess, Hannah Jason. But her enquiries threatened to unlock the cage where crucial secrets had long been held captive.

THE TWILIGHT MAN
Frank Gruber

Jim Rand lives alone in the California desert awaiting death. Into his hermit existence comes a teenage girl who blows both his past and his brief future wide open.

DOG IN THE DARK
Gerald Hammond

Jim Cunningham breeds and trains gun dogs, and his antagonism towards the devotees of show spaniels earns him many enemies. So when one of them is found murdered, the police are on his doorstep within hours.

THE RED KNIGHT
Geoffrey Moxon

When he finds himself a pawn on the chessboard of international espionage with his family in constant danger, Guy Trent becomes embroiled in moves and countermoves which may mean life or death for Western scientists.